ROGUE'S RENDEZVOUS

ROGUE'S RENDEZVOUS

Nelson Nye

Chivers Press • **Thorndike Press**
Bath, England **Waterville, Maine USA**

This Large Print edition is published by Chivers Press, England, and by Thorndike Press, USA.

Published in 2003 in the U.K. by arrangement with the author c/o Golden West Literary Agency.

Published in 2003 in the U.S. by arrangement with Golden West Literary Agency.

U.K. Hardcover ISBN 0–7540–8941–X (Chivers Large Print)
U.K. Softcover ISBN 0–7540–8942–8 (Camden Large Print)
U.S. Softcover ISBN 0–7862–4920–X (Nightingale Series)

The text of this Large Print edition is unabridged.
Other aspects of the book may vary from the original edition.

Set in 16 pt. New Times Roman.

Printed in Great Britain on acid-free paper.

British Library Cataloguing in Publication Data available

Library of Congress Cataloging-in-Publication Data

Nye, Nelson C. (Nelson Coral), 1907–
      Rogue's rendezvous / Nelson Nye.
            p.   cm.
      ISBN 0–7862–4920–X (lg. print : sc : alk. paper)
      1. Large type books. I. Title.
PS3527.Y33 R6 2003
813'.54—dc21   2002036017

CHAPTER ONE

Grimed and testy, with a rime of dried sweat showing white at the armpits, Jeff Kitchim pulled up to peer from disbelieving, beard-stubbled cheeks back across twenty yards of hoof-pocked road to find the girl still watching.

A provocative sight in her gypsy finery—scarlet, yellow and white against the mud wall of Arristo's Cantina. Slim, willow straight and tall for a gitana, though perhaps that high comb might account for some of this. Hair glimmery black as the sheen of a grackle's neck. Whitest teeth and boldest stare Kitchim had seen in a damned weary while; and he grinned at her, nodding, saw her thoughts close him out as, with lifted chin, she put back a hand to reach for the door.

Unexpectedly childlike, in the entrance she paused, eyes round as marbles, to appraise him again. Before she ducked out of sight, red lips pulled apart in a brighter flash of teeth, and there was nothing of a child in that gamin grin.

Kitchim, staring, swore.

Flirt with him, would she? He was minded, by grab! to go in there after her.

Jeff Kitchim had been a long time away from women.

1

Thinking tiredly back he scrubbed a hand across his face and, picking up the reins, kneed the floundering horse between flanking hovels. Everything seemed a long while, thinking back.

He felt about ten years older than Moses.

He'd never set out to become a hired gun. He guessed, halfway scowling, he had kind of fell into it. Impatient to get ahead, to have a spread of his own, he'd found orthodox ways too snail-like and slow. He'd courted quick money, and there'd been plenty of that available to fools.

No brains required. All a gun boss demanded to shell out fighting wages was a quick trigger finger and a scarcity of scruples.

Jeff had qualified early and now, at twenty-eight, was beginning to wonder if he'd backed the wrong horse. All across Texas the law was moving in. Owners who'd considered him survival insurance were lately finding Kitchim's presence embarrassing.

He hadn't encountered any dodgers carrying his particulars but that axe could fall anytime. Posted men were getting common as fleas and several who might recognize him were presently being whitewashed to pack Ranger tin.

Looking about, Jeff grimaced. Wasn't much of a place to come so far to get to. A manyanner town of flat-topped adobes—half of them unplastered. Only three miles north of the river's present banks. El Federico. Last

2

time he'd been through this country—five years ago—El Federico had been Mexican-held but now, since the Rio had gouged a new channel, the subsequent 'banco' on which the town stood had become, through treaty, a part of the sprawling Lone Star State. It was why he'd returned. What had happened once could happen again if the right kind of storm hit the river some night and this time maybe, if the cards broke right, he could make the big stake which had thus far eluded him.

Was that asking too much? Jeff Kitchim didn't think so on his hard-used horse. He had no other prospect if he couldn't make it here. Chancy? Of course—but he'd taken bigger chances for a whole lot less.

Striking south, toward the river, he rode with eyes half shut against the glare. The day's heat came out of the sandy earth in scriggly waves that danced like film against the gray-blue of faroff hills. There was nothing around him but pear and catclaw, and tatters of amber forage grass, and, here and there, sticking up the gray wands of wolf's candle or the gnarled dwarf shape of an occasional mesquite.

A lonely land. Hot and dry and, for the most part, forgotten, given over to cattle and coyotes and the legless snakes that were native to it—which was all right with Kitchim.

His tough cheeks reflected a secret humor as he peered around seeking landmarks to figure from, and angling his mount a little

3

more to the west.

In talk with others who had been through here he'd been told the new channel made a rather sharp loop around an outcrop of granite in this general direction, possibly two miles from town, and he wanted to have a look at this before getting down to cases with Fell.

He had already marked the river's old course with its straggly line of dying cottonwoods and willows—had even got down and tramped round through the stones below where the rampage had quit its last bed to gouge the new channel. It did not add a great deal to what he'd previously guessed. The river had left its banks at a bend.

One thing a man had to say for Kitchim—he was thorough, leaving nothing to chance which patience or hard work could bend to his favor. He had gained that much in these past nine years.

But there were facets of his character not easily bridled. The wild streak in him which had made him what he was still rebelled upon occasion, unsettling better judgments. That recklessness—at once his strength and bitterest weakness—was the albatross fate had hung about his neck, and it was this which had kept him chained to his rut.

Breasting a thicket of squatting cedars he came up in his stirrups to rake a long stare across the dun, heat-hazed miles. It had to be out there somewhere between his horse and those domes and spires, the ragged edges of slides, the gaunt outlines of chimneys and eroded bluffs lying red, chalky yellow and five shades of ocher against the gray shapes of those southernmost hills. He wasn't thinking now of the river but of the prize tucked away among these sunbaked wastes.

Biding on with his shadow through the late afternoon, cursing the heat and those lost younger years, he was forced once again to the hateful conclusion that his kind had outlived their use in this country and that, regrettably, guns were about all he knew. He had to make it this trip or bid good-bye to all hope for any better tomorrows. Had to make it now or cross the last thin line between what he had been and the sorry damn prospect of cashing in his chips at the end of somebody's rope.

CHAPTER TWO

He came down off high ground to tie his horse in the shinnery, afterwards peering through half-shut eyes to look rather grimly at the dream which had fetched him these many miles; the mud-brown river—sluggish now from months of drought but a roaring tiger in the time of rains, the tumbled rocks and parchment growth and beyond, the irrigated greenery of peon-worked fields and orchards

5

. . . the red-tiled roofs and bell tower of Luis Capistrano's Hacienda Bavinuchi.

A kingdom balanced on the caprice of a river. Bavinuchi was cattle and wool and hides, storehouses, stables, shops and barns, a village, an empire—*a ~~goddam~~ dam way of life*, Kitchim thought, staring in open-faced envy. Hell for the peasants but a heaven on earth for those who stood at the top of the ladder. A pearl beyond price, but the pearl could be his if he played his cards right and had any luck at all.

He'd remembered the look of it all these months . . . the stone saints and scrolls, the dusty plaza, the great house standing silent amid its garlands of flowers. The work office, commissary, farflung tangle of adobe corrals, the thick-walled quarters of Capistrano's mayordomo. The huts and shacks of the paisanos who toiled in ignorance even as their fathers before them had toiled among the hayfields and vineyards, the pens and pastures . . . wherever ordered to increase the Capistrano wealth and well being. A feudal empire—his for the taking.

Snorting, Kitchim wheeled back to his horse. His for the taking, but only *if* and *providing* quite a number of things. Not all of which, unfortunately, depended on himself.

Climbing into the saddle he stood up to stare again, then kneed the big dun down a cattle trail which wound through the brush in the direction of the river. The bank proved too

6

high at this point for his purpose and he was forced to ride west, well back from the crumbly rim, until the bluff toughened up enough to permit cautious passage. And thus he came presently to the bastion of granite about which the river had been flung, growling, north.

He could see at once that no amount of storms were going to break up any barrier as rugged as this—not, at any rate, within his lifetime. No wall of turgid water was going to leap this bend and he might just as well make up his mind to it. Acknowledging this, Kitchim turned his horse to look for other possibilities. And, backtracking, came within the hour to a curious convolution of the channel's tortuous course.

Kitchim, leaving the river, excitedly climbed to higher ground and dug the telescope out of his blankets. From this vantage, working the glass, he was able to bring Bavinuchi into considerably sharper focus, discovering the hint of something which he intended to examine more closely at his earliest convenience.

The purling curl of the Rio here, though dropped ten feet between mauled banks, was narrower, swifter, or swifter seeming, the southern face scarred and pocked with the unmistakable signs of erosion.

Thoroughly engrossed, Kitchim spent a probing while with glass at eye before abruptly closing and putting it away. The results of this survey occupied his cogitations for such an interval it was very nearly dark when the horse at last clumped him back into town.

Lighted lamps yellowly dappled the road's patterned shadows in front of the shops and strictly adult attractions. Kitchim turned into the first livery he encountered, glad to get down and stamp some feeling into his legs. 'Give him the best,' he told the gimpy Mexican who came up to take the reins. He paid in advance with a ten-dollar gold piece, waving away the change with a smile. 'Where's the best place to eat?'

'Tio Eladio's, patrón. Go with God.'

Half buried in the gloom of a dingy alley the place, when tracked down, looked anything but the sort of establishment he was hunting. Its closed plank door, indifferently illumined by a guttering candle in an ancient ship's lantern, looked about as inviting as a basket of snakes. Kitchim, after a single hard scrutiny, pushed it open and stepped watchfully in.

He saw a ratty-looking combination bar and beanery. Check-clothed tables flanked three walls. At the mirrorless bar three steeple-hatted hombres had their heads together. Two lesser men who smelled as though they lived with sheep held down a table with a plate of tortillas, two bowls of steaming chili and a mug apiece of cheap beer.

Kitchim, grimacing, walked on past and dragged out a chair over against the north wall

8

where there weren't any windows to distract his attention. He was, he realized, the only anglo in the place, and wondered what crossgrained impulse had prompted that hostler to send him around to this den of thieves. Ali Baba, he thought, would have felt right at home.

After waiting five minutes without anyone coming to see what he wanted he sent a hard stare at the wizen-faced barkeep and, when that got him nowhere, finally poked up a hand. Getting off his elbows the fellow, a hunchback, presently shuffled over.

'Your pleasure, *señor*?'

'Grub,' Kitchim said. 'I'll take whatever you've got ready.'

The little gnome, without comment, plodded away, pausing to poke his face through a curtained arch before resuming his stance behind the bar. Kitchim's glance rubbed again across the three conspirators.

Though garbed as vaqueros they looked a pretty ugly lot, particularly the middle one, a big-bellied man burned near as black by the sun as the string-held cloth patch which wholly covered his left eye. The man chose that moment to twist his shoulders and discover Kitchim's regard. Kitchim looked away but felt the man's baleful scrutiny burn across him like a fist.

A black-haired muchacha in a sleazy dress shuffled forward with his meal, Mexican of

9

course and as obviously hot.

As the girl clopped away it seemed the scowling bandido at the bar was leaving also. By stretching his ears Kitchim trapped two words from the departer's admonition to the pair left behind. The first was *quinto* which was Spanish for fifth; the other sounded like *guerras*, but the only connotation he could squeeze from this was that it might be something having to do with a war. With a shrug he choused his thoughts back to the river and, picking up his bone-handled tools, attacked his food.

Finishing, he got up, put a coin beside his plate and, without a further glance toward the pair at the bar, walked across to the door, pulled it open and went out.

A cooler wind was blowing through the blackness of the alley. Long training in trouble held him flat against the wall, poised body wholly still and all the restlessness of his nature funneled into this grim, prolonged attention, his ears exploring all the sounds of the night. This was what the years had done to him, it was the price Kitchim paid for continued survival.

Satisfied he moved, slipping quietly into the main stream of traffic which, at this early hour, was easily identified as one skreaking dry-hubbed wagon wallowing over the ruts of the road, a solitary horsebacker moving toward the lights of the general store, and a brace of hombres in big hats and cotton *pantalones* who had just staggered out of Arristo's, homeward bound, and consoling themselves with a *pulque*-inspired version of *Jalisco*.

They brought back the face of the black-haired girl and, except for his need to make sure of Fell, he might have stopped for a drink and whatever she had going.

He should have been more definite. He could easily have said, 'I'll see you at the stable,' but all he'd put in the note was: 'Good proposition. El Federico. June 21.'

Been nice to feel you were dealing with a friend, but fooling himself wasn't one of Kitchim's faults.

Tight-lipped and wary he slipped along through the dapples of lampshine and shadow, wondering how he'd locate the man. Fell wouldn't be shouting his presence from no housetops. He was the carefulest gun Jeff had ever run into.

Scanning the shop fronts, one eye peeled for an inn or a flophouse, Kitchim found himself nearing the hitched horse of the man who'd gone into the store.

Pablo Ruiz the sign said, *General Merchandise.*

He could let things rock along, he supposed, and Fell—if he were here—would probably show when and *if* he wanted in. That was one way to play it. But to Jeff's way of thinking there were enough loose ends flapping around

11

in this now.

He reckoned he was going to have to show himself, regardless. He hadn't really wanted Mattie Fell or anyone else, but having offered the guy cards he would prefer to know, before he stacked any chips, whether and how far he dared to count on the man. Fell was bastard enough, if he thought he could cut it, to take over the action. He could be in this store, or in the brush south of town, just grinning and waiting like a ~~god~~dam spider!

So why, suspecting this, had Jeff got in touch with him?

It was a question Kitchim had asked more than once over the antigodlin miles he had covered getting down here. The answer never varied. He had to have help in a thing big as this. He wouldn't have trusted anyone and Fell with his timidities—his predilection for caution, looked the best bet available.

Jeff had worked with the son of a bitch before and forewarned was forearmed—at least he *hoped* it would work out that way.

He was just preparing to step into the store when a man said behind him, 'Like to talk to you a minute.'

CHAPTER THREE

There was a curt civility in the tone, nothing more.

Every muscle cramping, Kitchim forced himself to face around with a casualness he hoped might conceal the urges clamoring inside him.

There was no one on the walk, but through a door, not six feet away, he met the look of a man enthroned beside a desk, a balding man grown fat behind the star that glittered from his shirtfront.

He was not merely big, he was huge, colossal, a hogshead of a shape with arms like hams and legs that strained the fullness of his pants, so larded with flesh as to seem thick as gateposts. Everything about him was round, his elbows and even the balls of his knees. The white hair of his beard and the fringe round his head fluffed like the silk about to burst from a milkweed and—notwithstanding the double-barreled gun athwart this caricature's lap—Jeff's first impulse was to laugh and go on. But that was before he collided with the stare.

There was nothing about those eyes that looked humorous. Resettling his stance Kitchim, wiping the incipient grin off his mouth, growled: 'You talkin' at me?'

The old grafter's look, dropped to Jeff's belted waistline, came up with a hardening interest. 'Well, well, well!' he wheezed, stare flattening. 'Another pistolero.'

Kitchim threw out a look of polite inquiry, striving behind this—not liking the tone—to hatch up some story which might reasonably account for a stranger's presence. It was not helped much by the crusty inspection digging into his face with the sharpness of gimlets.

With a rumbling huff that tossed the beard about his cheeks the badge-toter demanded, 'What's goin' on at the ass-end of nowhere to fetch s' much trash up outa the bushes? An' never mind the lies—I've heard 'em all!'

'Why would I lie?' Kitchim said. 'Only reason I'm here is to get across the river. Any law against that?'

The old hypothecator heaved and gasped like a boil of lava about to send up a smoke. He got red in the face, appeared to choke on his fury, but before he could get his talk box to working a voice yelled from black depths beyond bars: 'Don't yammer, you fool! *Light a shuck an' git out of there!*'

While Kitchim stared, stunned, the shotgun moved off its bed of fat just far enough to give Jeff a look down its gullet. Both hammers went back with audible clicks.

The star packer grinned when Kitchim summoned a parched smile. 'Caught ye flat-footed, eh? Be smart an' stand still. The mess

14

this thing makes don't hardly bear thinkin' of.'

They considered each other through a dragged-out quiet. Weighing Jeff's look, the marshal nodded. 'Betsy here's a sure enough caution; you done right t' think twice. I'm Marsh—Oggie Marsh,' he said, hugely grinning. 'Ain't in no hell-tearin' rush t' git acrosst, be ye?'

Behind frozen cheeks Jeff's mind was jumping like a boxful of crickets. It didn't make sense for Fell to be in this jug but it had been Fell's voice which had yelled that warning.

He said, undecided, 'Well, I *had* sort of figured to lay over for the night . . .'

'Come in—come in!' Marsh wheezed, waggling an arm at him.

Kitchim would have preferred to remain where he was but with that cocked Greener balefully ogling his belly it didn't hardly seem as though he had much choice.

Not at all happy he stepped gingerly over the threshold, still wondering about Fell, about what the man's predicament might do to his plans.

Marsh, eyeing him fondly, pawed at his beard. 'We got a lot of laws here you mebbe ain't caught up with . . . laws about guns.' He paused, eyes bland, a little grin fluttering back the beard from his teeth.

It was Jeff's turn to nod. 'But naturally, as marshal, you could look the other way.'

15

'I could tell straight off,' Marsh said with approval, 'you wasn't no common run of drifter. I'm the J. P. here besides bein' marshal. How much loot you got on you right now?'

Strangling his resentment Kitchim emptied his pockets on the slide Oggie Marsh pulled out from the desk. Coins—gold and silver, a folding knife with two three-inch blades, a stub of pencil and a bullet-bent concha. Fully aware of the marshal's scowl he stepped back.

'What else you got, feller?'

Kitchim, shrugging, spread his arms.

'You *walk* in here?'

'Not quite. I left a wore-out horse at the Bon-Ton Livery, if that's what you're drivin' at. Its howcome I figured to spend the night. I got a brush-scarred saddle and a rifle. An' that's it.'

'Fifty-four forty!' Marsh's eyes, adding coins, thinned down to a gimlet stare. 'You tryin' t' buy a lawman with peanuts, boy?'

'Not trying to buy anything. You called me in—'

'That's *your* story. I could tell it some different.'

They stared again at each other, Kitchim's eyes bitter, the marshal's skeptical with hidden lights back of them a man couldn't fathom. In a disgruntled rumble thinly tinged with satisfaction he declared: 'Court's in session. What handle do you go by?'

16

Jeff, scowling, said: 'Kitchim,' but Marsh's look didn't change.

'All right, Kitchim. You been picked up on sev'ral counts. How you plead—guilty?'

There were a number of things Jeff was minded to say but while he stood glaring, Oggie Marsh, clearing his throat, leaned forward to wheeze: 'That jasper you heard right after you come in has had two more weeks spliced onto his hitch. F' talkin' outa turn. You thowin' yerse'f on the mercy of this Court?'

Kitchim, assessing his own plight, nodded.

'Then I'm inclined t' be lenient,' the old walloper beamed. 'Charge of packin' firearms inside the town limits carries a penalty of fifty dollars or two weeks in the pokey—I take it you ain't hankerin' t' spend no time in jail?'

'Take the fifty,' Kitchim said, and disgustedly watched Marsh count out and pocket it. He was moving to pick up the rest of his belongings when this outsized Roy Bean of El Federico set a fat finger down upon the folded knife.

'The charge of carryin' concealed weapons inside town limits is punishable by a fine of fifty dollars, one month at hard labor, or both,' he pronounced, reaching up around the grin to gently smooth his fluffy beard.

Jeff could feel the hot blood pounding into his cheeks and, clenching his fists, had half opened his mouth when, remembering Fell, he

17

had the wit to close it.

'You fixin' t' be in contempt of this Court, boy?'

Hanging onto himself Kitchim shook his head.

Marsh pursed pink lips, considered his victim and with a great air of tolerance rather ingeniously declared, 'I suppose, bein's you're so anxious t' git acrosst the river—an' in view of your straightened financial condition, it would be a act of Christian fo'ebearance if this Court was t' let you go. Providin' we kin reach a amicable agreement about this here fine . . . ?'

Behind the hard clamp of locked jaws Kitchim nodded.

Marsh's bright little eyes from their ambush of wrinkles appeared to weigh him again. 'Truck ye got left on that slide ain't negotiable. Horse,' he said in a tentative teasing sort of tone, 'from what I been told ain't scarcely wo'th more'n thirty . . . guess the Court could allow ye fifteen. How says the pris'ner? Speak up, boy!'

'Done,' Kitchim growled.

'Bridle, saddle, blanket an' rifle would mebbe fetch twenty-five—if a man had ary use fer 'em, that is. Considerin' theah condition Court'll hold 'em at ten an' no hard feelin's. You figgerin' t' balk?'

'Afraid that's a luxury I can't afford.'

The old grafter chuckled. 'Glad ye see

18

which side of the bread gits the butter. Now let's see what we got. Totin' up I reckon we've took care of half of it.'

Like some great fat toad in his tiny puddle Oggie Marsh reared back on his homebuilt armless throne of a chair as though, by God, he was maharaja of Hindustani.

Kitchim trembled with rage.

Marsh, grinning, waggled the shotgun. 'You wanta throw in that shell belt an' pistol?'

Kitchim, glaring, stood silent and seething, bitterly aware the way this was going he had no more choice than a hooded falcon. No man in his fix could beat a cocked Greener. He snarled in frustration. 'I can see you're bound to hogtie me, regardless—how long am I in for?'

Marsh clucked over him like a mother hen. 'This Court,' he wheezed, 'is partial but fair, seekin' on'y t' carry out the letter of the law. Mistuh Kitchim, suh, you're not *in*—yet.' Sighing, the old reprobate declared, 'Just t' prove this Court's not unmindful well give ye the benefit of the "warlike intentions" charge—an' if that ain't bendin' over back'ards I don't know what is. Knocks a full ten dollahs off yo' fine. Court'll take belt an' pistol f' the rest of yo' obligation—just pitch 'em on the desk an' ye kin walk right out.'

Suspecting a trap, afraid the man's blithe heartiness was no more than front for some cruel trick, Kitchim peered hard at that mountain of flesh before, with fingers he could not quite keep from fumbling, he unbuckled the rig and with considerable reluctance tossed it onto the desk.

Someway managing to keep his lip buttoned he was wheeling to go—was actually in mid turn—when Marsh's hateful voice, reaching whispery after him, inquired spider soft, 'Ain't ye about t' be fergettin' somewhat?'

Lividly—speaking through clenched teeth-Kitchim said, 'You're expecting *thanks*—'

'Wouldn't know what t' do with it—or them,' Marsh replied, flapping a hand at the belongings still littering the desk's pulled-out slide.

CHAPTER FOUR

Jeff Kitchim stepped into the lamp splashed street feeling like a skinned rabbit and so buffaloed and wild he could not have hit the ground with his hat in three throws.

In a towering rage he struck off for the place where he'd put up his mount, thinking no further than to get on him and go, ringy and blind enough to lash out at anything. But inside half a block the churn of his passions had sufficiently eased that he could see the foolhardiness of trying to get away with a horse the law had confiscated. It could very well be what Marsh was hoping he'd attempt.

Considering Fell's plight it seemed not unreasonable to suppose El Federico's enterprising marshal might have a standing arrangement with the livery's proprietor to pass along the word whenever a stranger tried to bail out his horse.

Opening his fist Kitchim glared at the slither of coins on his palm, the grubby stub of pencil and the bullet-bent concha which was all Marsh had given him the leave to walk out with. He was minded to pitch the whole works into the street but, glowering, dropped the change into his pocket and, finding himself in plain sight of Arristo's, went catty-cornering over to see what inspiration might be dredged up out of a bottle.

Without a gun he felt naked as a jaybird, all his customary coolness completely out of reach, that experienced cleverness of knowhow and tact as remote to present need as though by God he'd never been in a bind!

And he hadn't—not like this one, vulnerable as a kid in three-cornered pants. Someway he had to get hold of a gun!

It was the only coherent thought he had time for as he moved through the room's smoky light toward the bar. A swarthy long-haired character in cotton *pantalones* was off in one corner teasing a guitar; the place, even at this early hour, had a pretty fair sprinkling of customers mainly, it appeared, of the boot and saddle variety. And here, again, it seemed he was the only person likely to be considered a *gringo*.

Several wenches with trays were flitting about in their swivel-hipped fashion among the clots of steeple-hatted males as Kitchim, hugging his bottle, pushed away from the mahogany. He was elbowing his way toward a vacant table when his scowling glance chanced to light on a face he had all but forgotten in the throes of his dilemma. Her eyes were following him with the same bold interest he'd observed in her before.

Kitchim stared. The girl's red lips pulled away from her teeth and he was hooked, moving toward her, all else discarded in the electric impulse which drew him unthinkingly as flame draws a moth.

She was younger than he'd thought, the discovery almost stopping him until, reassessing the quality of her regard, it became pretty obvious she was inviting his attention, wanting him to come over—daring him to try his luck. He forgot all about the turn it had taken in the urge of old hungers.

Gypsy or Mexicana her features, though fine, were too boldly fashioned for the current trend in beauty. She had, despite her astonishing slimness, all the right curves provocatively distributed, but these were only a part of her appeal, having little to do with the irresistable compulsion that was hauling him nearer. Rather, he thought, trying to settle it later, it was the eyes that grabbed him, something glimpsed in their brightening depths—more challenge than promise, that fetched him across the room to her side.

Not until he'd come up to the table, still peering, half scowling in his trancelike absorption, did he realize what he might be blundering into. The girl was not alone—she had a lot of man with her, the big-bellied ruffian with the black-patched left eye who'd been talking with the pair at the bar in Tio Eladio's, the place where Kitchim had taken his supper. This bull-chested fellow was not pleased to find himself sharing her attention with a strange and boorish *norteamericano*. Nor was he at all adverse to letting Jeff know this. Nor was the girl unaware.

'*Pobrecito,*' she sighed, gaze intent, lips stretching. 'I'm theenk the great seizer 'as made your acquaintance.'

Kitchim ruefully grinned at her allusion to the marshal. 'Afraid he has,' he admitted, unable in the baleful glare of her companion to find a more suitable reply. While—glance still locked with the girl's—he was trying, the affronted bandido, or whatever he was, surged from his kicked-back chair with an oath. A hint of stained teeth showed behind the twists of a bristling mustache.

'*Basta*—enough!' he cried, fiercely waving Jeff off, hand plunging swiftly to grab at a

23

knife protruding from the sash wrapped about his bulging gut.

There was no time for choices. Kitchim, unarmed, let drive with the bottle. The man staggered back with blood on his face. The girl, in a flutter, shoved Jeff toward a door. '*Vamanos*—go! *Hurry!*' she gasped; and Kitchim, swearing, found himself stumbling through the trash of an alley.

Panting, off balance, pushed by the sudden cold fingers of panic, he floundered perhaps another five strides before the night wind, blowing up from the river with its smells of dank earth, pulled him back from the crumbling edges of folly. Stopped, grimly listening, he scanned his chances, and moved with caution toward the alley's mouth. More than ever he felt the need of a gun. With a gun and a horse he could be gone from this place, hidden deep in the brush till he could think what to do about Mattie Fell. And, of course, Bavinuchi.

He guessed, a little bitterly, he was going to have to steal them, and it came over him the marshal had probably reached the same conclusion—was likely waiting, even now, to catch him in the act.

But the night was filled with risks and if he were not gone before that business in the cantina came to Marsh's ears he would likely end up behind the same bars with Fell. Black Patch wasn't going to forget this, either, and might even turn out to prove more dangerous than Marsh.

There was no good going to the stables for a mount; that was one place certain to be under surveillance. His best chance, it looked like, was to bide his time and snatch one from the tie-rails flanking the shop-fronts.

Muscles bunched, eyes narrowed, Jeff eased into the street, seeing nothing inimical in that first sweeping glance. There was no commotion pouring out of Arristo's, no appearance of excitement anywhere along the street. Drawing a freer breath his quartering stare swiveled over the racks in a widening astonishment. The only horses in sight were bunched, all four of them, tied to the rail in front of Ruiz's Mercantile.

Kitchim didn't like it. It didn't seem natural. It had the smell of a trap.

The feeling of danger rushed all through him, sweat making a dry prickery stinging along his cheeks. Rooted in shadow he heard a dog yap somewhere. Looking longest at the horses he pondered the street with a solemn care while his pulses thumped and wind blew the cloth of his shirt against his chest. He watched a man come out of the store, anchor his purchases, step into a saddle. And he watched that man ride off up the street through a crisscross of lamplight, turn onto the range and jog off, heading north.

Bitterly murmuring, Kitchim saw no other

course but try it. If he waited here long enough they'd all be gone. He speared a bleak look at the dark front of Marsh's office and the spurless strike of somebody's heels coming over the walk, bounding back off the shopfronts, pushed him out of his crouch . . . into reluctant, irretrievable motion.

CHAPTER FIVE

Drifting away from the alley—holding to this casual pace while each stretched nerve thrummed its terrified protest—Kitchim, with the drawn blank cheeks of a gambler, cut over the lifting dust of the street.

You might never have guessed what turmoil seethed behind the locked clamp of that rigid mask—the shock and dread, the cold clawing fears, the scheming, discarding, hoping desperate stab of wildening eyes as, partway across, Oggie Marsh, with his shotgun, stepped into a splash of light from the store to stand, widely grinning, by that rack of hitched horses.

It was too late to run. There was nothing Jeff could do but go on with a growing sharpness to all his angles while the dogged tramp and sullen rasp of spurred boots took him hopelessly into this confrontation.

And so, rocked to a stop, emptyhanded and filled with the spleen of his bitterness: 'Marsh,' he said, 'what've I done now?'

'That kin wait. It ain't s' much what you've done, d'ye see? as it is that my town's bein' prowled by a drifter.' Now the piggish eyes gloated. 'A vagrant, a bum without money or prospects—'

'Look! All I want is a chance to get out of here!'

'You had a chance, Mistuh. I turned ye loose once. How many hints does a guy like you need?'

Kitchim's fists were so tightly clenched they ached. 'All right,' he said, 'I'll get moving straightaway.'

The fat grin nodded. 'That's fer sure.' The shotgun leveled. 'Move into my office.'

Sweat stood damply on Kitchim's tipped face and bound in the cloth stretched across hunched shoulders, shining in the creases that rimmed his pinched mouth. Hate boiled in his stare. The marshal hugely enjoyed it.

'Step careful now—march!'

Finding no help for it Kitchim's shoulders dropped. A great breath fell out of him and he was turning to comply when a cool voice called: '*Minuto uno, señors.*'

Jeff stopped in his tracks. He'd no idea where she'd come from but it was her, all right, the black-haired *gitana* he had left in Arristo's. Scorn thinned the red lips and the arrogant look of her narrowed the marshal's stare to pale slits.

'Now looky here—' he began.

She paid no heed to his bluster. 'W'y 'ave you arrest thees man—eh? Tell me that!'

Marsh heaved and huffed, his great face with its fluttery hair turning crimson. 'Am I the marshal of this place or ain't I?'

'Thees man—w'y you are putting heem in your juzgado?'

''Cause he's a bum, that's why! No-good! A vagrant!' Marsh wheezed and huffed as though about to strangle. 'A ~~goddam~~ trouble huntin' puffed-up drifter without no visible means of suppo't—'

'Supote? W'at ees that?'

'Means he ain't got no money—no *dinero*! No job!'

'Oh, but 'e 'as!' The girl's eyes laughed above the curl of red lips. 'Ees the man of Don Luis. The new pistolero Bavinuchi 'ave hired to keel off the . . . the how you say—t'iefs? W'at 'ave take so much cattles.'

The marshal looked like a stabbed baboon.

Disbelief, consternation and a whole miscellany of less readable emotions jostled and stumbled over the man's gaping features.

Kitchim was some astonished himself, hard put to imagine what had fetched her up with such a notion as this, but liking it too as his mind leaped ahead and an outraged conviction winnowed down through the star-packer's flattening stare.

He didn't ask where she'd got this or how

she knew. With his jaw snapping shut and the fluff fanning out about the grip of his mouth like seaweed caught in a gigantic wave, Oggie Marsh with his look turned as flat as a wall, wheeled the heaves of his girth like some harpooned leviathan and went wallowing off in the direction of his lair.

Kitchim didn't laugh. He didn't even grin with the thought of that baleful face sinking through him. Certain as death and taxes was the shivery hunch that Marsh wasn't done with him.

The girl touched his arm, brought him back to the present.

'I'm powerful obliged to you, ma'am,' he told her, and saw the bright lips slide away from her teeth.

'*De nada*,' she said. 'Good luck—you 'ave *caballo*?'

'Horse?' He shook his head.

'A leetle corral ees behind the cantina. Take the *moro* and—*vaya con Dios*.' She squeezed his arm and was gone like smoke in the shadows.

Go with God she had bidden.

With a shake of the head Kitchim let out his breath and, still pondering her words, cut back over the street and reentered the alley. Cautious now with his footing he inched his way through smashed crates and stacked barrels, testing each step among the rubble of discarded tins and emptied bottles, still not knowing what to do about Fell.

He could hardly afford to write the man off.

It didn't seem probable Marsh would keep him penned long. He would have to be fed. The thinnest slop wasn't free, and from what Jeff had seen the law of this place would have small patience with anything taken from that side of the ledger. And there'd be hell to pay if Marsh found reason to suspect a connection between his prisoner and the gunhand hired to hunt wolves for Bavinuchi.

That girl was no fool. Leastways there was nothing slow about her wits, coming up slick as slobbers with a windy neat as that. She had sure saved his bacon! Snatched him out of the frying pan cool as you please, and if there was anything back of that yarn she had spun . . . What outfit that big didn't lose a few cows? If they were losing enough—Might be just what he needed if he could make them believe it.

He found the pen, and there were two horses in it. He spent five sweaty minutes talking under his breath to them before reaching up to get the hackamore off the horn of the saddle and slide, pulses thumping, between lower bars.

The scarcity of maneuverable space helped considerably. He caught the blue roan without too much fuss and, just to be on the safe side, soon as he'd got the gear piled on he took down the rails and hazed the other horse out. Swinging aboard the blue then he listened, ears stretched, for any hint he'd been discovered. Somebody was still plucking tunes from a guitar but, except for an unexcited murmur of conversation, this was all he could pick up.

It was no time to linger. Eyes wide and quartering Kitchim eased the hide into a carefully held-down walk, moving him into the deeper dark behind buildings. When brush closed around them Kitchim, breathing a lot freer, pointed the gelding's head toward the river.

In this kind of light it was not too easy to locate a crossing and the best part of an hour slipped away before he found one. Some of this time he spent on his plans, overhauling them somewhat in the light of recent developments. But the girl was never wholly out of his thoughts. He was uncomfortably aware of an undercurrent here, an unwanted premonition that closer acquaintance might prove not only brash but quite possibly downright dangerous. Yet, over and beyond anything he might owe her was the girl herself, turning him unaccountably restless, loosening restraints imposed by cooler judgment.

He tried to hoot away the craziness of notions all too obviously preposterous, laying most of them to abstinence, reminding himself she probably had a dozen lovers and that nothing but trouble could come of seeing her again. He had a stake to make in this country and had damned well better be about it. But the thought of her stayed with him.

He came out of the water perhaps a couple of miles northwest of Bavinuchi headquarters, the frog and cricket chorus thinly bothered in the distance by the barking of a dog. He was clear of Marsh for the moment and had better catch what rest he could; time enough tomorrow to call upon Don Luis.

Night's chill was setting in when he got out of the saddle in a motte of mesquite, hauled the gear off the horse and turned him loose on trailing reins. There was some chance he might lose him but better this, he reckoned, than be caught with a staked-out stolen hide.

He beat the ground with a stick to scare off snakes, gouged a place for his hips and finally stretched out on the sandy earth, covering himself as best he could with the blanket, using the saddle for a pillow.

But his mind kept working, dredging up things far better left lost. The pull of that black-haired witch was working through him and nothing he tried quite put her out of his thoughts. She was still peering at him as, at last, he fell asleep.

The sun was two hours high when the warmth of it woke him.

He threw the blanket aside and got up with the rifle to have his hard look through the stickery branches. Nothing moved in his sight but the horse browsing yonder several hundred yards away.

Even with the riata off its owner's saddle Jeff stalked that coy damned hide clean back to the river before the bastard would step into a loop. Very near wild enough to work the brute over, Kitchim, hand over hank, walked up the rope to stand within feet of that reared-back, ugly, eye-rolling head and all, by God, he could do was glare.

This horse had endured a whole lifetime of hate and had the ridged scars of abuse to prove it. It wasn't just the scars or that stubborn defiance that held Kitchim rigid as something hacked from stone, but the mark, like a skillet of snakes, burned into the left hip—the brand of Bavinuchi.

CHAPTER SIX

Evening shadows stretched gray fingers long across the powdery earth when Kitchim, with the heat curling round him like flames, glimpsed again through green branches the hacienda's pink tower. Not, this time, from the direction of the river but from the baked yellow trough of a canyonlike valley which, coming out of the west, lost its crumbling southern wall to become open range as it debouched past the bench housing Bavinuchi's buildings.

It was this which yesterday had so engrossed him while peering through the glass above the Rio's Texas bank, the kind of thing he'd hunted, a bed for raging storm-driven waters. Satisfied now, still aboard the captured roan, he had come to pay his call on Don Luis Capistrano, a gringo astride a stolen Bavinuchi horse.

It got the attention he'd expected.

Through the ferny jade lace of palo verde and huisach he saw the arrested shapes of peons staring in mingled astonishment and fear as, slouched in the saddle, he rode up the lane to stop before the entrance arches and iron-grilled gate, waiting quietly in the quietness. He was a tall man drawn and bony in hunger, sitting a blue horse that did not belong to him with the sweat dripping off his hawk's nose and scarred chin and his half shut eyes bright as cut glass in their insolent survey of the armed guard with spurs and the wolf-faced cur that came sniffing and snarling to circle the legs of this bridleless mount.

'If you value the dog, hombre, get it away from me.'

The armed man, scowling, resentfully fingered his antiquated pistol, peered again at the horse, hurriedly crossing himself before he pulled up his jaw in belated remembrance of his authority. 'Over there—' he grumbled, spitefully turning to kick at the dog before lifting a pointing hand. 'Over there is the place

34

of the man you look for.'

'I look for Don Luis.'

The fellow stared. 'Are you mad?'

'*Por qué?*'

'You think the *patrón* would talk with a gringo?'

'He'll talk with me,' Kitchim said, 'if he cares for his cows. Look at me, hombre! Go tell what you see—and don't forget the horse.'

Dubious, but impressed, the man went into his box and somewhere a bell set up a rusty jangling while Kitchim, considerably less assured than he seemed, embarrassedly listened to the rasp of his breathing. The bell broke into its racket again. A hatless peon came running from a row of mud shacks.

Beckoned inside by the guard they held a muttered conversation, both men several times looking up to scowl through the bars of the box's tiny window. Presently the peon in his cotton *pantalones* disappeared up a path between trees toward the house.

The guard came out and, with thumbs hooked over the rim of his shell belt, lounged against the plastered mud of his box. Like the sullen yellow eyes of the scrawny dog his roving stare examined a multitude of things while never quite touching the cause of his disquiet.

Kitchim found little humor in the guard's uncomfortable silence. He had his own worries, having thought at some length about

35

the risks he would run riding up to this place on the horse between his legs, accepting those risks because he found no way around them. No one who was anybody in this country ever went anyplace afoot. Besides, with luck, this stolen horse might lend credence to the part. Meekness here held neither promise nor virtue.

Then he saw an old man striding gateward through the splotches of darkening foliage, the peon at his heels awkwardly armed with an arquebus and looking as though at any moment it might bite or explode him into some dreaded hereafter.

Thin and straight, his back like a ramrod, the old man stopped to peer through the gate. Thick gay brows crouched above that bleak stare while the guard straightened into some semblance of attention. 'A bold one, this,' the old man said, concluding his inspection. A tuft of iron gray hair bristled from his chin and the eyes above that line of clamped mouth revealed nothing. 'What do you want?' he said curtly.

'My business is with the *patrón*,' Kitchim stated.

'Then speak, man. I am the owner of this place.'

'Don Luis?'

'The same.'

'And do you make your business the property of the wind to fly where it will across the face of the land?'

The heavy brows drew down in anger. The hacendado coldly smiled, waving his guard and his peon aside. 'Did you come here in your effrontery expecting to extort an agreement of pay in return for a promise to stay away from my cattle?'

Kitchim, matching his scorn, said over curled lip, 'I can see that kindness has small value here.'

'Kindness, *señor*?'

'I considered it a kindness to return a lost horse.'

'The horse was stolen. Let us not play—'

'I know nothing of stolen horses, old man. This one I picked up without bridle twenty *kilómetros* south on the road from Laguna Guzman.'

'And what made you think it was mine?'

'By the brand—how else?'

Don Luis considered him in skeptical silence, mouth tight with the held-back things he was thinking. 'And of course you expected to be paid for your trouble—'

'Only,' Kitchim said, 'if we came to some arrangement having to do either with the return of your cattle or the apprehension of the persons who have made a business of stealing them.'

Something faintly grudging showed in the old man's stare. 'Set a thief to catch a thief. Is that your proposition?'

'I've been called worse than that,' Kitchim answered, staring down at him. 'I don't think it's likely I can get back the cows. I *can* undertake to stop the persons responsible.'

'For some pieces of silver you would turn on your own as Judas did Christ?'

'Old man,' Kitchim said, 'I didn't run off your cattle.'

'How did you know I had lost any?'

Kitchim sat a moment regarding him, temper tightening the turn of his mouth. 'I'll be taking this horse for my trouble. Good day to you!'

'Anger makes a foul supper. You would not get off this place on that horse—'

'Don't bet on it.'

Their eyes clashed and locked. Neither pair pulled away.

The hacendado sighed. 'Who hires a thief may wake up a pauper.' He grinned, suddenly saying, 'Man, what do I call you?'

'My name is Jeff Kitchim.'

The old don's eyes held amused disbelief. 'No matter,' he said, and clapped for his henchmen. 'Pablo,' he told his peon, 'take care of the horse,' and, to Kitchim: 'Report to the foreman of vaqueros, Jeff.'

Kitchim, throwing a leg over the horn, dismounted. He felt the jibe, all right, but he hated to see that rifle get away, yet could hardly protest without diminishing his stature. He had a strong urge to lunge for it when his lifted glance found Capistrano grinning.

Kitchim flushed and stood there, rooted, while the peon led the horse away. He felt the guard's stare, heard the old don chuckle. 'Better arm yourself, hombre.'

Kitchim said angrily, 'You want the men shot?'

'I want them stopped. For this I will pay fifty pesos—each one. How the affair is accomplished is no concern of mine.' He turned without further words and strode off through the green blobs of foliage.

The guard went back inside his Turkish bath.

Swearing under his breath Kitchim struck off through the weeds toward the clutter of shacks with his rumbling gut and his hatful of worries. His lack of a weapon was acutely embarrassing but, at least for the moment, he was on Bavinuchi, the man of Don Luis, a hired pistolero entitled to be fed. More, he was where he wanted to be—thanks to the lies told Marsh by that gitana. Maybe the foreman would have a gun he could borrow.

A barefoot girl was quartering over the dust toward one of the hovels as Kitchim emerged, sleeving his face, from the weeds. He called to her. She paused, the brown eyes regarding him with open curiosity, a strange gringo without a gun or horse but with the spurs of a caballero.

'The foreman of vaqueros, *señor*? *Quien sabe?* Over there . . . that is hees house.' She stared without comprehension, a look that said, *But aren't all gringo crazy?*

'Who shall I ask for?'

'Teófilo,' she said and fled.

Kitchim's glance touched the corrals. They were empty, save for the Bavinuchi roan he'd come in on. He dropped down in the shade and put his back to a post, tipped his hat over his face and took what rest he could.

He awoke in the dark to the racket of horses. Several men, booted and spurred, were noisily hazing them into a pen. He stood up, tiredly stretched, discovering a light in the shack pointed out to him.

Cuffing some of the dust from his pants with his hat, he put it back on and, feeling his hunger, headed for the light.

He knocked and stepped back. Heavy steps came toward him. The door was hauled open and the foreman stood, a monstrous shape, in the lamp glow.

Kitchim knew at once he'd get no gun from Teófilo. For this—black patch and all—was the man from the cantina he had hit with the bottle.

CHAPTER SEVEN

Many things passed through Kitchim's head in that moment. Recognition was mutual, both sides of the door, nor could there be any doubt of Teófilo's reaction. A tremendous pleasure spilled into his face and this savage satisfaction brimmed the whole look of him as one hand went back to get hold of his knife.

'Wait!' Kitchim cried. 'I have orders from Don Luis!'

The man's burning eye never left Kitchim's cheeks nor did the look of it change, but the hand came empty away from his sash. The great chest muscles bulged as he twisted for leverage and the hand blurred out, fisted, to explode in Kitchim's face. And he went flat on his back in the ground's yellow dust.

Desperate, he rolled to avoid chinging boots, and someway got up onto his feet only to catch another clout that sent him sprawling. Teófilo, grinning, chuckled deep in his throat, hugely waiting while Kitchim, head ringing, got one wobbly knee under him and, finally, gasping, fulcrumed himself into some kind of stance.

The big-bellied walloper's left fist languidly lifted and Kitchim, twisting to duck, took a right across the mouth that spun him halfway round. He backed off, shaking his head, and glimpsed the ring of dark shapes, the avid Mexican faces that, hemming him, ruled out any chance of escape.

He was caught without hope in the gun fighter's nightmare, trapped without weapon against a barroom brawler who had everything going for him, reach and know-how, at least forty pounds and a memory which . . . Jeff clenched his teeth. He'd be lucky if this fellow didn't cripple him for life.

The big Mexican was a quicker man than Kitchim. Despite the belly, Teófilo's ability was evident and the grins of the watchers held no doubt of the outcome. He struck Kitchim twice on the head and laughed as the American went staggering around like a blinded calf. *'Mirar, gringo!'* A flying fist took Jeff in the chest and flung him backward against the massed men. With yells and shouts they threw him back into the man, sledging hard as he could at the foreman's thick middle.

It was like beating a drum and did no good at all. Someone gasped and the world became a pinwheel of lights and Kitchim's knees turned to water. All the breath whooshed out of him and, before he could fall, there was a kind of hard tug, all motion was reversed and his jerked-open eyes found him stretched at arms' length above Teófilo's head. The foreman, turning, put him into a twirl—faster, faster, and then he spun through the air. He heard someone dimly give out a great cry, and found himself floating down a black spiral that appeared to have no discoverable end.

$$*\qquad *\qquad *$$

It was the darkest, weirdest night he could remember, and the longest, most uncomfortable one. Through all those strange hours unrelenting devils kept assiduously at him, prodding and rolling, wrapping and unwrapping, cutting and tieing, as though he were a bundle being readied for Christmas, all the time talking some outlandish gibberish, freezing him, roasting him, ignoring his pleas, deaf to his curses—doing in fact about everything imaginable to keep him from getting the rest he needed. And the lights! By God there must have been two hundred of them, hovering about like a gang of poor relations at the reading of a will!

He got it doped out that most of the time he had probably been dreaming, maybe delirious a little. The first thing he knew for sure he was on his back in a rope-sprung bunk on a pile of scratchy blankets framed by four gypsumed walls and mighty little else. Drunk! he thought, drifting off again. He seemed to have an impression of soft cool hands passing over his face.

The next time the white walls floated into focus, his quickened glance took in the window, a tiny, many-paned affair through

43

which a hot wind was blowing from a day that was just about shot.

Struggling onto an elbow he discovered he was naked, and his mind groped to grasp what hotel he'd gone to bed in—a pretty crummy place he decided, peering about. Then his glance found his clothes, all washed and clean again, on a packing crate over at one corner. More mystified still Kitchim flung off the blanket to swing feet to floor—a *dirt* floor, by God!—and that was when the pain hit, oozing from every joint. He braced himself, gasping, all the bones in his body feeling like they'd been poleaxed; and he fell back, groaning, in the shake of a sudden chill.

The place was gray with shadows when, gingerly, he managed to push up again and, panting, chanced a look at himself, staring in clammy wonder. That hadn't been all dreams and delirium. Someone had sure as hell worked him over, and they hadn't missed much. From neck to knees he was purple-green splotched with a profusion of bruises he was open-jawed eyeing when something tugged his glance to the door.

It stood widely ajar, blocked by a shape whose beefy face brought everything back like a drench of cold water.

Teófilo said, 'Tomorrow you work or get off thees ranch.'

Kitchim worked. From dawn till dark in a dreary succession of interminable hours he wrapped up every bastardly chore the man threw at him, hatefully, bitterly biding his time. He had no idea what had happened to Fell. He could still be in jail or gone from the country; Jeff had no way of knowing and scant time for wonder. Teófilo delighted in finding the roughest, most danger-fraught jobs for him, and always there was someone keeping tabs. Never was he left unwatched for more than a handful of minutes—not even at night. This surveillance chafed like a saddle sore, the more since any pay he might earn must derive entirely—under the terms of his presence— from the apprehension or killing of cow thieves. Apparently in ignorance the foreman left him no time for poking around. Only one good thing, aside from toughening him up, had come out of this plethora of backbreaking peonage. A working grasp of Bavinuchi geography and, to a lesser extent, some idea of the deployment of riders.

Four days passed in this frustrating itinerary, Kitchim eating with the unmarried cowboys in a kind of barracks-like mess hall a stone's throw south of the pink-towered chapel. Turning out of the place now with Domatilio Vargas, the close-mouthed man assigned by the foreman to share quarters with him, Jeff was warily astonished to find Teófilo waiting.

The boss vaquero wasted no words. 'You are wanted at the house, hombre. *Andale!*

Pronto!'

Passed through the gate, discouragedly wondering if Don Luis expected a progress report, Kitchim approached the massive shape of the hacienda's big house, feeling a wind coming up off the desert, hearing the cottonwoods rustle overhead, seeing the dark shapes of the *tabacón* leaves, keeping to the gravel. He came up to the front and swung around on the flower-bordered path that led off to the side and a proper entrance for peons, paid help and others not socially acceptable, and then said, 'To hell with it!' and, going back to the portal, pounded on the door.

It was opened at once and by their expressions it would have been difficult to say which was the more astounded, Kitchim or the girl who stood framed in the opening.

She looked breathlessly frightened and Jeff, shaken too, imagined for a second he was out of his head again. He couldn't help gaping. Black of hair as that snake-hipped witch of Arristo's cantina . . white teeth too, same color of eyes. But that one's eyes had been bold and inviting as the lure of red lips and off-shoulder blouse which had taken him into that clash with Teófilo.

This was a girl raised for better things whose regal bearing, rich dress and shocked stare spoke of blood so blue it could have no acquaintance with thrown bottles and bars and

46

the other wild things which connected her up in Jeff's mind with the girl who had talked him out of Marsh's clutches.

Confused, taken aback, he dragged the hat off his head like the rest of the paisanos when confronted by one of the dons or their women; and then, flushed in resentment, was opening his mouth when, with hand at throat, she cried, 'Why are you here?'

Kitchim suddenly grinned. 'You do not recognize the man of Don Luis? The paid pistolero—'

'You fool!' she whispered. 'Get out!'

CHAPTER EIGHT

Kitchim, turned stubborn, stepped inside and, grimly considering her, shoved the door shut. 'I don't know what kind of game you're playing but its plain enough you wanted me here—'

'I did not send for you! *Madre de Dios*, do you think I am *loco*?'

'In town . . .' he began, but she stormed through his words breathing scorn and fury. 'In the town ees not here! Do you imagine my father—'

'All I know is Teófilo said I was wanted at the house.'

'Teófilo . . .? Does he know,' she said quickly, 'you are here about the cows?'

Kitchim shrugged. 'Don Luis may have told him. He don't know it from me.'

She stood there chewing her lip, lost in thought. He said, 'What difference?' and then remembered the surveillance, how filled with work his days had been.

'I asked for a rider.' Her tone was worried. She raked him with a searching stare. 'Why would he send *you*?'

'I'm a rider.'

She considered him doubtfully, lip caught in teeth again, a remote speculation stirring back of her eyes. She said, 'You don't understand . . .' then pushed it away from her. 'It's my father.' Fright came into the dark search of her glance. 'He needs a doctor.'

'What's the matter with him?'

'His side, I think. He talks . . . different—he can't use his right arm.'

Stroke, Kitchim thought, and narrowed his eyes at her.

She said, breathless, 'El Federico.'

Jeff got the message. Marsh, of course; she was bothered by what the marshal might do to him. But Marsh, first of all, would have to lay hands on him, and Kitchim had no intention of repeating the blunders which had trapped him before. 'Chances are he won't . . . Where do I look for this pillroller?'

She gave him directions, said nervously: 'Wait—' and came back with a pistol, a single shot .50 caliber pocket gun, a weapon much in

48

vogue among the gambling fraternity. 'Take this,' she said, pressing it into his hand, 'and— be careful.'

He should have gone at once but, slipping the belly gun into a pocket, he kept hold of her hand. With the smell of her hair unsettling his thinking and the wide searching eyes of her so darkly there just in front of his own, the crazy notions set loose got through his guard and he pulled her against him.

'Please . . .' she gasped. 'Don't . . .' but he smothered her struggles, pursued the twist of her cheeks until her mouth, finally captured, lay under his own. She quit squirming then and Jeff, finding no resistance, kissed her again, and once more for good measure. Turning loose of her then with a satisfied grumble he yanked open the door and plunged into the night.

At the pens he roped out a dark bay without blaze, tossed a blanket across it and was just cinching up when Teófilo's spindly shanks and burly shoulders came out of the dark with a challenging '*Quien es?*'

'Kitchim,' Jeff said.

'What are you doing with that horse?' the man asked in Spanish.

'I'm off to El Federico.'

'At whose orders?'

'The *patrón's.*'

The foreman of vaqueros, completely still, regarded him. 'What does he want?'

'*Un medico.*'

Teófilo, sounding suspicious, said, 'For whom?'

'He did not confide in me.' Jeff picked up the reins and the big foreman, grudgingly, allowed him to pass.

Kitchim led the horse out and swung into the saddle, feeling the stab of Teófilo's regard. But all the man said was, 'Make a quick trip of it and don't lose that horse.'

Kitchim pointed the bay toward the river. Now, by God, he'd find out a few things! Then he thought of the girl and patted his pocket. A don's daughter. 'Damn!' he said, remembering the feel of her. But, crossing the river, more important considerations took hold of him, and the look of Marsh's eyes, flat and shiny as fish scales, stirred an increasing uneasiness in him.

Understanding border politics he could find more sense in the marshal's turning loose of him, now that he knew the girl was Don Luis' daughter. Just the same, he reckoned, he'd be wise to get the doc and recross the Rio soon as possible.

But there was Fell to consider, the man's part in Jeff's own plans, the scheme which had fetched Kitchim into this business. He had not given up the notion, was more set in it than ever, and a few ideas had turned up during the days he'd spent as Teófilo's private peon.

Yet he still felt the burning need for a gun—

50

something more than the toy in his pocket which he considered to be worthless beyond ten feet. Something with more than one load in the barrel, something that would stop a man beyond the range of Marsh's Greener. Nor was Kitchim forgetting that Bavinuchi foreman.

Kitchim thought—everything considered— Teófilo had been just a little too restrained this evening. Almost as though, behind the gruff tone, things were falling into place in a way that secretly pleased him . . . and the girl had said she had *not* asked for him but only for a rider.

Why had Kitchim been picked?—a man Teófilo had been watching like a hawk? Had there been more to that beating than a blow from a bottle? Had the foreman found out or someway guessed the reason this gringo was riding for Bavinuchi? The girl had voiced that thought, too. Had the boss vaquero smugly imagined he had just said good-by to a dead man?

There was food here for thought and Kitchim, leaving the bay to pick its own gait, chewed and rechewed it with increasing disquiet. He recalled the unsavory pair he had seen with the foreman in the bar at Tio Eladio's—that talk of *quinto* and *guerras*, and wondered what day of the month this was. Wondered, too, if there were any connection between Teófilo and El Federico's gargantuan badge-packer. And while his suspicions were traveling apace Jeff asked himself also what the daughter of Don Luis—garbed and be-baubled like a girl of the Ursari Bear Tamers—had been doing hanging around Arristo's cantina. It would bear looking into, he was sure enough of that.

But with the gun-slinging brethren first things came first, and only a fool ever looked behind. One way or another a man's mistakes were mostly written off in gunsmoke—as Jeff's could be were he to figure this wrong.

Eyeing the lights of the town he decided first of all to get hold of another gun; time enough then to go look for that sawbones. And if the old man worsened it was no skin off *his* nose. Might be better all around so far as Jeff was concerned. Bavinuchi might be up for grabs, and with an unmarried daughter . . .

Kitchim smiled a slow smile and turned his attention to conning the night. The girl he could handle. He had better make sure he could take care of Marsh.

Two sources of guns, both risky, were available. The rack at Arristo's where men hung up their weapons in accordance with Oggie's ordinance. And the mercantile which, if closed, he could burgle.

Under other conditions he would have chosen the latter, but it was cheek by jowl with the marshal's office, so he cut off through the brush to come up behind Arristo's.

No mounts had been left in the little pen

tonight. Swinging down Kitchim snubbed his Bavinuchi horse to one of the poles, securing the reins with a slipknot on the off-chance he might care to leave in a hurry. Ignoring the door he had departed by, remembering the rack had been against the front wall, he worked his way through the alley's trash, stepped up onto the walk and lounged against the dive's front while narrowed eyes went skittering through the street's blue-black shadows.

Nothing untoward there. The mercantile was dark but light splashed the walk in front of Marsh's office. If there *was* any connection between Marsh and Teófilo, or if the foreman had sent Oggie word that Jeff was coming, nothing Jeff could see gave this any support. If the mercantile's darkness was in aid of a trap Kitchim wished Oggie joy of it and, pushing open the door, stepped into the cantina.

Six or seven steeple-hatted drinkers were holding down the bar with perhaps that many more scattered around among the tables, and off at one corner the long-haired kid in the cotton *pantalones* was singing of unrequited love while mauling the strings of his homemade guitar. Jeff did not notice any significant attention.

With an appearance of nonchalance he paused by the rack, face settling into a tighter clamp when, looking them over, the only thing he saw even relatively modern was an indifferently cared-for single-action .44 holstered to a battered belt whose loops held less than half their complement of cartridges. Reaching for this he heard the door open back of him, could feel the harsh stab of the newcomer's stare.

It was too late to get any good out of turning. He clapped the belt round him, jerking the tongue through its big silver buckle, carrying himself in three strides against those fellows at the bar who stood, eyes sprung with horror, watching over his shoulder the loom of catastrophe.

'Hei, Pito!' rang the marshal's high yell. 'Grab him—*grab him*!'

And a man's chin came round, one of the pair Jeff had seen with Teófilo. But this chap, with Jeff's pocket pistol ready to take his everlasting picture, wasn't grabbing anything.

CHAPTER NINE

This, when the chips were down, was one who could think. As Jeff brushed past, bound for the door he had left by before, near the bar's far end, the fellow thrust forth a foot.

It threw Kitchim hard but he kept hold of his pocket gun and, as three others dived for him, fired point blank. One man, twisting in mid-air, screamed. The others, eyes enormous, went stiff in their tracks as Jeff, bounding up, slashed back a hand for the stolen pistol.

It was gone from the holster, spilled in his fall. 'Bavinuchi!' he yelled, and threw the empty pocket gun across the room in a glittering streak just as the marshal was bringing up his Greener.

The shotgun roared but Jeff was down, scooping up the pistol, careening round the bar. The place was a bedlam as he crashed through the door.

Outside, the night wind cold against his streaming cheeks, jerking loose the reins he got a foot in the stirrup and, oblivious to racket, had the horse in a hard run before he touched saddle.

Straight south he rode, pounding loud for the river, the bay's ears flat to the sides of his head. Not till the brush closed round them did Kitchim slow, and not even then for another five minutes of branch-popping progress. He wanted no doubt about where he had gone, for the moon was up now and he must still return to get hold of that pillroller. And more important than this—to Jeff's way of thinking—was the honed-sharp need to know what day of the month this was. He could not leave that lay with the foreman, Teófilo, grown so large in his mind.

When he picked up the shine of the river he swung west along the near crumbly bank, glance lifted, hunting with sweat-stung eyes for a crossing; turning back, when he found one, in a northerly quartering; walking the horse, all his senses alert; seeing the shape that rose out of blue shadows, throwing his gun on it, holding the hammer ready under his thumb. 'Careful, now! Watch it!'

'That you, Kit?'

It was Fell with both arms stiffened over his head.

Jeff pulled up, staring down at him. 'Marsh turn you loose?'

'Three days ago.' Fell, lowering his arms, began a bitter cursing. 'No gun, no horse, no ~~god~~dam money—'

'You'll have money 'fore we're done with this.'

'It better be plenty. If you could seen the slop that sonvabitch fed—an' not a mouthful since but three-four gophers! ~~God~~dam gut thinks my throat's been cut! I owe you a lot, man.'

Kitchim, eyeing that glowering face, said, 'What day's this—what day of the month?'

'Who cares . . .?' Fell began, said gruffly: 'Fourth.'

'*Guerras* ring any bells with you?'

Fell's gangling frame quit its restive flutter. The bony shoulders tipped, the narrow chin came up to show the rust-red of his hair where the moon touched. Out of this staring, his grumbling voice, softer now, said, 'Up the river a piece there's a town of that name. I come

56

through gettin' down here—'

'How far?' Jeff said.

'Ten mile, mebbe. What's Guerras to do with us? That where this dough is hid?'

Kitchim explained his deal with Don Luis, then told of seeing Teófilo and those other two at the bar that night in Tio Eladio's. 'I caught two words, *quinto* and *guerras*—'

'An' come up with it's this foreman that's liftin' the cows, eh?' It was plain Jeff's companion was a long way from sold on it. 'You pull me here for a two-bit play?'

'I don't know what Teófilo's up to—revolution, maybe, but he's sure up to something and better be stopped if your idea in coming was to leave with full pockets. It's Bavinuchie—place he's foreman of—that I've got my eyes on.'

'Your eyes, eh? What's that supposed t' mean?'

'Means I expect to take over—'

Fell's bitter laughter cut him off. 'Bavinuchi? What kinda stuff you been smokin'? Bavinuchi!' he snorted. 'Why'n't you jest figger to lop off Chihuhua!'

Kitchim lifted the reins. 'It's no job for weak hearts.' He kneed the bay into motion.

'Here,' Fell growled. 'Wait!' and caught hold of the stirrup. 'Never said I . . .'

Kitchim, stopping the horse, grimly eyed him. The man looked what he was, a tiger-faced Texan who got his living with a gun and was good enough with it to command top pay. But there were plenty of others and Jeff, rubbed wrong, brought this fact to Fell's attention. 'I could have passed the word to Beal, or Carrondaga; I could name an even dozen who'd have jumped at the chance to partner the man who grabs Bavinuchi. Nobody's forcing you.'

'Hell, I'm in. It's just . . . a man likes t' know where he stands . . Bavinuchi's *big*. How can two guys—?'

'You know what a banco is? Ever read the treaty our rough-ridin'. Teddy cooked up with Mexico? Provides that whenever, wherever, a chunk of land, big or little, is lopped off either the U.S. or Mexico by reason of the Rio Grande changing its bed, that chunk shall henceforth be a part of the country on whose side of the river the new channel leaves it. Which is how El Federico comes to be a part of Texas—savvy?'

Mattie Fell broke suddenly out of his tracks, eyes stretched wide, the whole look of him incredulous. 'You think Bavinuchi's goin' to jump them banks?'

'With an assist from us—with a little help— yes.'

Fell shook his head. 'I git out from under my hat to your gall.'

'Well? You in it or ain't you?'

Fell, narrowing his eyes, let the stillness run, scowling at the concept, rasping the palms of

58

his pretty hands together, irritably growling as one then another of the risks caught his notice. 'How we gettin' past the rest of it—even if the river decides t' do what we want? Damn little of that stuff in El Federico—'

'The worrying is *my* job. All I need from you is a kind of touchy help, and I haven't got the time to argue about it now. Yes or no?'

Fell, uneasily frowning and—like Jeff before him—still woolling it around the darker corners of his mind, was unable to resist the picture painted by cupidity. 'Yes . . .' he said and, skewered by Kitchim's stare, finally pulled his mouth together.

Kitchim watched him a moment longer. 'You can drop out of this right now and no hard feelings—'

'Said I was with you, didn't I?'

'All right,' Jeff said, describing the hard-faced pair who'd put their heads with Teófilo's by the bar where he'd first seen them—Pito and the other. 'Arm yourself and get over to Guerras. See if you can locate one or both of them; just find them and sit tight. I'll see you there tomorrow. Be around and be ready.'

He touched the horse with his spurs.

He was moving at a walk when he came in behind the town's mostly dark buildings and quit the saddle to stand deep in silence a hundred yards back of the doctor's mud house, thinking mostly of Fell while he listened to the night and lengthily considered the immediate surroundings. The wind had dropped but there were no crickets chirping. The quiet breathed over his nerves like they were harp strings. Farther back, under tamarisks at the townward end of the house, something moved.

Looked as black, off there, as India ink. No gleam of lamp came through the doctor's windows; only way to make sure was go up there and knock. There were several notions scriggling around behind Jeff's stare, but setting up a mark for Marsh's Greener wasn't one of them.

Something told him to stay away from there.

He could go back of course and claim the doc had been out of town. The girl would have no way . . . but that damned foreman might! He may have ridden in himself hoping to catch Jeff in something he could use to be rid of him. He might have sent another hand. He might have let Marsh know Jeff was coming across the river, but the marshal hadn't known he would flush Jeff when he stepped into Arristo's or he'd have made a better job of it.

A man could speculate all night and never butter any parsnips.

Kitchim could feel the run of sweat across his cheeks. His mouth turned small and grim as his glance reached again across the moon-blued shadows, appraising that deeper dark beneath the trees. If a man was over there—if it weren't just some strayed cat or prowling dog it could as well be Fell as anybody else.

Jeff hadn't mentioned the sick don or told Fell where he was bound for, but this did not preclude his having learned from other sources. He had only Fell's word for it the man didn't have a horse.

Kitchim cocked the gun he had taken from the cantina and, fed-up with waiting, started carefully toward the house.

CHAPTER TEN

Hung over the town in argent splendor the lopsided moon seemed bright enough to read by. Away from the horse, caught full in its glare, he had almost reached the point he aimed at when the rhythmic scrape of shovel against earth sent him into a spread-toed, frozen crouch.

Who in the name of Job's lost ox would be outside digging at this damned hour?

The sinister rasp of it was almost certainly emanating from some place beyond that westernmost wall—the town end where tree gloom was deepest . . . about where he'd thought to have glimpsed something move.

He couldn't think why the steady slither and tump of this clandestine shoveling should bring into his mind the black-patched face of the burly foreman but it was there, darkly smiling in the oddly pleased look that was the last Jeff had seen of him. He remembered the girl's 'Does he know you are here about the cows?'

Kitchim, growling, was against the house when he happened to recall it was Marsh she'd looked afraid of, and he wondered again what she'd been doing at Arristo's. He made a twist in his thinking to ask about that and then, spider soft, he was rounding the corner, staring, scarce breathing, through a swirl of stirred shadows at the bent, blacker shape leaning over the shovel.

'Strike a light,' Kitchim spoke, gun leveled from the hip.

Without flurry the man slowly pushed himself erect. 'I can see—'

'Strike a light!'

With a sigh the man reached into his discarded coat, got a lucifer block from a pocket and scratched one.

Kitchim softly swore. Whatever he'd imagined he would find it wasn't this. The fellow—a man Jeff had never before encountered—had been setting out what looked to be rose cuttings and tulip bulbs. 'Kind of funny time—' Kitchim began. The fellow snorted. 'Man in my line of work's lucky to find *any* time! What with buryin's and birthin's . . .'

'If you're the doc,' Kitchim said, 'you're wanted at Bavinuchi.'

The old fellow, grumbling, picked up his

coat. 'Ain't no one chopped off his tassel has he?'

'It's Don Luis. From what the girl said I expect he's had a stroke.'

'Been courtin' one long enough.' Doc twisted his head. 'Don't seem to remember comin' across you before.'

Kitchim shrugged. He put the pistol away. El Federico's pill man said, 'How'd it effect him?'

'Well, she said—'

'*Who* said?'

'The girl—'

'Some of 'em, maybe, ain't got a pot to piss in but they've all got names, an' there's half a hundred of 'em—which are you talkin' about.'

'Capistrano girl.'

'Daughter, eh?' Jeff could feel his eyes sharpen. 'She's got one—Meetah. Prob'ly comes from the Spanish; Amita, I'd guess.' Held by a finger he had the coat over a shoulder, leaning on the shovel while he toted Jeff up and couldn't seem to be satisfied.

'What's the chances,' Kitchim asked, 'of His Nibs kicking the bucket while we're lallygaggin round here shooting the breeze?'

Tossing the shovel aside, nodding, Doc said, 'You do have kind of a pins-and-needles look. Prob'ly need more greens in your diet. Can he move everythin'?'

'My job's cows. Girl says he talks funny, having some trouble with one of his arms.'

Doctor stared a breath longer, bobbed his head again, clucking, 'No rush I'd say. You'll find ol' Frannie in the shed off yonder. Get a saddle on her, will you? I'll fetch my bag.'

*　　　*　　　*

At Bavinuchi the guard passed them through without comment. The moon had moved over some. It must have been about three but there was light in the house. A moza opened the door before Jeff could knock and took them gray-faced through a shrub-prettied patio to call at a door off a flower-banked gallery which Meetah threw open to beckon in the doc.

The servant withdrew and Kitchim, left to himself, strode about for a bit, hardly noticing what he looked at, winding up finally staring into a fountain bubbling out of piled rocks and cattail-like growth behind a drinking iron deer and a pair of cast ducks.

He found his thoughts clumsily jumbled. Why had the marshal turned Fell loose? To cut expenses? Cut his losses? Or as decoy for some kind of fishing expedition? A wily bird, that Marsh, a grafter sure, but a deep one, a sharp one with a nose honed for profit. Had he already sniffed a connection between them and turned Mattie loose to prove his suspicions? Had he only just happened to step into Arristo's when Jeff had been lifting that gun from the rack? Had he been told to expect

Jeff, warned perhaps by Teófilo?

It seemed plain as plowed ground the Bavinuchi foreman was up to something, certainly. Tomorrow at Guerras, if Fell did his part, they might have a few answers Jeff could use to better his standing, perhaps even to institute himself here permanently—or for as long, anyway, as it suited his purpose.

There was a shorter route he could take he thought sourly. He hadn't known about the girl when he had first shaped his plans. He wasn't partial to double harness—had been lone—wolfing it too long, he reckoned; but marriage would certainly improve his position—might even dispense with his need for Mattie Fell, whom he trusted even less than he could this don's daughter.

He turned at her step. She looked troubled in the starshine and stopped beyond reach to stand in silent appraisal, watchfully weighing him, reminded no doubt of his proclivities and strength. He grinned at her, wryly. 'The bad penny returns—didn't you think I would, Meetah?'

'Where did you get the belt and pistol?'

'What were you doing at Arristo's that day?'

Her tongue went over dark lips thoughtfully. 'A trade?'

'Why not? The hardware came from the rack in Arristo's.'

'You just helped yourself? No one objected?'

65

'It got a little sticky but I got clear in one piece.' He told her about it, briefly stating the facts. ' 'Fraid I lost your artillery.'

She shrugged this aside, continuing to eye him with that dark speculation stirring again across her cheeks. The doc, coming out of her father's room, approached them. Seen more clearly he was big shouldered, bandy legged, better suiting the role of country deacon in his lifeless black, pale shirt and dark tie. He stopped with chin lowered, studying them from under shaggy brows. Hatless now, head gleaming in its baldness, he showed a broad nose, mouth wide lipped but caustic.

'He'll keep until morning. Reckon you'll want me to sleep here—'

'Of course.' The girl clapped her hands. 'Will his arm . . . ?'

'Depends. Probably I'd say, if there are no complications. That side of him's partly paralyzed, but if we can keep him stationary, keep down excitement, I would think he'd be up and around before long.' He considered her a moment. 'Don't suppose you could guess what brought this thing on?'

She looked at him doubtfully.

'He been worryin' about anything?'

'We've been losing some stock.'

'Cows? Yes, I see,' the doc said, glance swiveling to Kitchim. The moza came up, Meetah explaining his needs, and he followed the girl off, leaving the pair of them alone again. Kitchim said, 'And now . . . about Arristo's?'

'I was watching for you.'

Kitchim's smile was thin, disbelieving. He shook his head at her.

'It's true,' she said, and pulled up her chin. 'For someone *like* you, at least. Someone quick with a gun.' She said, nervously watching him, 'You have learned something, haven't you?'

It was Jeff's turn to shrug. 'Bit early to tell—'

'But you have your suspicions?'

'I've got a passle of them. What,' Kitchim growled, 'took you there the second time—to Arristo's, I mean . . . when I found you at that table?'

'But I've already told you.'

'Looking for a gun fighter?' Kitchim narrowed his eyes at her. 'How many grab-an'—shoots you figurin' to hire?'

'But how could I know you were going to come over here?'

He considered her look of childish astonishment. 'And the gypsy get up—you always wear that when you step down to deal with gringos?'

Even in this blue light he could see the stain of color that pulsed into her cheeks, the tightening mouth, the flat and faroff look she raised between them. 'And Teófilo,' he said, throwing in the rest of it. 'You two looked pretty cozy—'

She slapped his face and stepped back, breathing hard. 'I do not have to answer your questions or account for your cheap stupid gringo suspicions!' Indignation burned through her stare, and she whirled in a flutter of skirts and was gone.

CHAPTER ELEVEN

Finally done with scowling after her, Kitchim let himself out and returned to the mud box in which he shared sleeping space with Domatilio Vargas, the bird dog Teófilo had detailed to keep tabs on him. The bunks were built one above the other and both of them were empty when Jeff, shedding clothes, climbed into the upper.

Bone weary, he expected sleep to elude him. Too many things were spinning round through his thoughts, suspicions and worries for which he had no sure answers. He seemed each year to tire quicker, come back slower and take less joy in the things he did. This was part, he guessed, of the same harsh truths which had fathered the conviction that he had to make it now if he would make it at all. Bavinuchi, if it didn't take care of him, could damn well be his Waterloo.

He woke, filled with aches from his twisting and turning, to a room black as soot, crammed with a kind of listening stealth that had frightened away all the insect sounds and left in their place a kind of pulsing dread that could only come from the nervous stab of unseen eyes.

With a straining care—not otherwise moving—he felt around for the pistol he had got into bed with. As his hand closed upon it— as he was bracing himself to throw off the blanket—the jerk and rasp of the nerved-up breathing grew still then bounced into a jumpety off-key whisper. *'Jefe!'*

Kitchim, swinging both legs over the side, snarled, 'For Chrissake! Ain't you no better sens'n to come in here?'

He could see her now against the thinning gray of the slot-like window built in without glass. 'You want to get me shot?' he growled, hugging the blanket and wondering uncomfortably where the hell Vargas was.

'I had to come—there's no one . . .'

'Even the ⬛⬛dam night has *eyes*!'

'It's not night now; in ten minutes it will be daylight.' She drew a shuddery breath. 'They've gone!'

'Who's gone?'

'The vaqueros . . . the ones, anyway, that were quartered near you.'

Kitchim, dropping onto the floor in his blanket, still gripping his gun, peered through the gloom at her, thoughts racing and edgy. 'How do you know?'

'I've been watching for this—I heard them! I saw them!'

'How many?'

'Perhaps a dozen . . . It's Teófilo, isn't it?'

'When?' he said.

'Perhaps two hours ago—maybe three. Is Teófilo . . . ?'

'Probably.' They'd be heading for Guerras if he had this pegged right, for Guerras with cows. And if Fell didn't spook them . . . 'As boss vaquero,' he said, thinking aloud, 'the guy wouldn't have much trouble laying out work to give the ones with him all the chance they'd need to move and have ready any she-stuff they wanted. All bred, of course.' He pulled the chin off his chest. 'If they've been making off with any sizeable bunches how come nobody's tracked 'em down.'

'Teófilo has been the one to go after them. Always, he says, the tracks disappear.'

Kitchim, nodding, said, 'They probably do. There'd be some of the men, anyway, he'd have to fool.'

'But you think you can find them?'

He wondered at the eager-anxious way she put the question. Man would almost think the purse was hers they'd come tumbling out of. He had closer things to think of, wasn't paying much attention to her gabble. He should have insisted her father put the deal in writing . . . what if the old man decided to renege or, after Jeff had this licked for him, refused to believe

70

his own range boss was guilty?

She put the question again, both tone and look demanding an answer. Kitchim checked the drive of his temper, saying dryly, 'It's been generally my habit to do what I set out to—'

'Take me with you,' she said, and it hauled him out of his thinking to stare.

The light was good enough now that he could see she had dressed for it. She caught the uncharitable cut of his glance. 'If it turns out to be Teófilo,' she urged, 'you may be glad to have someone to substantiate your side of this. An impartial witness.'

He scowled at the inference. But she could very well be right. It wasn't clear to him why he didn't want her with him. There was Fell, of course, the risk of stray bullets . . . the need to take Fell over the ground. He knew these were only excuses. But without going into the thing any deeper it was all too apparent he hadn't much choice. Unless he cared to turn the girl against him.

He concealed his reluctance behind expressed pleasure, sent her off to get saddled while flinging into his clothes. Women! he thought. There were only two kinds. Good ones and bad ones. And this was the knowledge that kept disturbing his judgment, feeling the pull of her, thinking how easily . . . worriedly resenting her ability to unsettle him, knowing he ought either to ignore her completely or bend every effort in the direction of marriage. She could be charmed into it. Hadn't spurned his kisses had she? A masterful man was just what she needed.

And such a union, he realized, had everything going for it, obviating the perils of depending on Fell, making wholly unnecessary the sweat and fragile planning required for bancos and changed channels and the subsequent adjustments which, so far, he hadn't even gone into. Intimidation, open belligerence, would be the best answer probably for any adjusting once the hacienda had been removed from Mexican jurisdiction.

But adjusting a sick and frail old man was one thing. Intimidating Meetah, backed by half a hundred reckless vaqueros, could be something else again; and the first imperative in any event was the permanent removal of that rogue Teófilo. There'd be no reconstructing that one.

So—on to Guerras.

But he could see the sense in making it appear they must rely on tracks—all the trumpery of signs and signal smokes—if they were to come up with the robbers' destination.

They set forth in the first rosy tint of dawn. Meetah had been impatiently awaiting his appearance at the pens with saddled horses and a bewildered ragtag of six armed peons, bandoleered and barefoot, shy—even embarrassed, in this unprecedented situation.

Eyeing them Kitchim almost threw up his

hands. 'If we've got to have help,' he had growled disgustedly, 'why not take some of your *regular* riders?'

He'd seen her head snap up, the rebellious detail of darkening cheeks, so he was not too surprised at the way she lashed back, declaring that in the first place none of Bavinuchi's regular riders were about and that, all things considered, nobody with the wits of a half-grown goat could afford to put any trust in them anyway unless—in Jeff's wisdom—he could point out the loyal ones.

Bridling under what he took to be sarcasm, seething at having to endure this from a chit of a girl, Kitchim, jerking a nod, went up into leather, grinding his teeth on the need to snap back, scarcely able in spite of this to keep his lip buttoned.

It was not hard in a tucked-away section of river bottom to pick up the sign of moved cattle surcharged with the marks of shod and ridden horses. Nor was this difficult to follow through several oblique shifts until, around noon, the pushed cattle came into a region of malpais, a dark basaltic lava choking out all vegetation save occasional sparse clumps of cottony looking bunch grass. This rusty rocklike covering, sharp in many of its edges and easily displaced where individual pieces were sufficiently small to turn under the scuff of hoof or boot, appeared extensive and was, Kitchim knew from personal experience of the stuff in other places, hell on beasts and practically impossible to follow anyone through.

He had no intention of attempting to track either the robbers or the stolen Bavinuchi cattle across so desolate a stretch. They'd have a sore-footed herd in mighty short order if they went for any distance into this kind of country, nor could he believe Teófilo would be so foolish. He'd stay with it just long enough to bury his trail, coming out at some place easily missed by any who might seek to follow. Jeff, with his chips on Guerras, took a long dreary look at this black chunk of country and—not averse to increasing his stature—waved the peons disgustedly away from it.

He could feel the girl's stare but, giving her never a glance, choused his sweating paisanos off toward the river which, invisible from here, ran almost at right angles to the apparent direction being taken by the herd. The girl continued to fume in silence for perhaps as much as a couple of miles. When he still showed no sign of swinging back toward the malpais, she reined up beside him, demanding, quietly furious, to be told what he was up to.

'Was kind of figuring,' he said, 'to lay hold of Teófilo—'

'And you think he went *this* way?'

'Don't you?' Kitchim asked, knowing damn well she didn't. Then, before she could answer, he threw in as though this settled it: 'Since any chance I've got of bein' paid depends on stopping him, I expect you'd better take my word for it.'

'The word of a pistolero!'

Kitchim's glance flashed thin and cold. 'Ever wonder how you'd fare if your friend with the patch took over Bavinuchi?'

He enjoyed the look that leaped into her face. He did not attempt to shove her nose in it, but rode off through the frightened huddle of peons to take over the lead with a saturnine grin, content to let her find her own level, deeming her too smart not to come up with the proper comparisons. Her with a stricken dad on her hands, a big hacienda whose riders she dared not put any trust in, a foreman she thought was stealing her blind.

Kitchim felt, by God, like he was king of the May.

CHAPTER TWELVE

They came, two hours later, back onto the tracks of the stolen cows, the paisanos and the girl giving forth with gratifying sounds of astonishment. Kitchim was too much up on his toes to show any flavor of out-and-out patronage, but in the smile he threw back at her there was just enough smugness to darken her cheeks.

Ten minutes later he cut away from the sign, angling north and east, wholly aware of her frowns, pleased to know he'd got to her again. And sure enough, after a spell of fuming in silence, she came cantering up with her anticipated questions.

'Well,' he said, dragging it out in a drawl, 'it should be pretty apparent we're moving faster than they are. They may or may not have an eye on the backtrail; in any event we'd be fools to engage in a fight we might lose. They'll be a lot more careless when they get where they're going.'

She was watching him with mixed emotions, trying the fit of these thoughts on her tongue. Then, giving him a penetrating look, she said scathingly, 'I'm to understand you've figured that out, too, and will get us there in time to lay a trap?'

'I'll do better than that,' Kitchim grinned. 'I'll recover the cows and nail Teófilo. How do you want him, plain broiled or parboiled?'

Her stormy glance appeared to find him insufferable, was probably halfway hoping he would come a cropper if only to prove him a windy braggart.

'And where do you think to do all this, hombre?'

'How's Guerras sound to you?'

Her eyes turned wide then flew out across the view, coming back to his face like dubious doves. 'About as likely,' she snapped, 'as your ridiculous boasts!'

'Care to place a little bet?'

The walking horses moved perhaps a dozen strides while she chewed at this interspersed with stabbing glances. The confident look of him appeared to give her pause. She said at last, uneasily, 'There's no railroad at Guerras . . . no way to dispose of cattle.'

'So what are you afraid of?'

Her eyes, suddenly dark as bits of smoking sage, suggested her pride could not withstand the taunt. Up went her chin. 'What sort of bet, hombre?'

'If this comes out the way I said, Bavinuchi's going to need a new boss of vaqueros. I want the job.'

'You *do* think big, don't you? And what happens if this fails, if you don't save the cows or catch Teófilo? Or it turns out to be someone else?' she said scornfully.

'In that event you can write your own ticket.'

She looked considerably tempted. 'What have you got to lose?' he scoffed. 'You can't run cows without a segundo. I came onto Bavinuchi in the first place because, by your tell of it, you'd been haunting that dive in search of a gunswift.'

Her eyes rolled away and came resentfully back. 'A pistolero without pistol?'

'I didn't have a gun when you talked up to Marsh. It was *you* put it into into my head to

77

see Don Luis. I suppose you settled for the best you could find. And you could hunt a long while without—'

'Spare me your boasts, gringo. You would sell a cat for a hare, I think,' she declared with a continuing slanchways look. A faint flush touched his cheeks, but he kept the tough smile on his lips, and the teasing taunt of this finally jerked out of her an angry nod.

'A-a-ai-hé,' she said. 'While the grass is growing the horse could starve. I accept your terms. If one is not to eat the stew who minds how it be cooked?'

There was something in the way she flung out that last which left him vaguely disquieted, but in the main he was satisfied he'd come a big step forward. If he could rid himself of Teófilo now and return to Bavinuchi as boss of vaqueros he'd be in capital shape for achieving his goal.

They sighted Guerras around four and found it scarcely larger than El Federico, a collection of mud hovels, a crooked street, a general store, a leather worker's shop, a twelve-by-twelve *carcel* for the housing of overnight prisoners. The largest building of all, and directly across from the jail, Jeff observed, housed of course the business of satisfying thirsts.

From a ridgetop perhaps a thousand yards away Jeff considered the town and laid out his strategy. The peons, he decided, should remain out of sight until they saw Don Luis' daughter in front of the cantina, at which time they would approach in pairs, one from the west, one from the south, and one from the north. At the limits of the town each man was to conceal himself and be prepared to stop anyone who appeared at all anxious to take himself elsewhere.

When he was satisfied they understood and would make some attempt to carry out these instructions, Kitchim with the girl moving in from the east, jogged their tired horses toward the center of town, swinging stiffly down in front of the cantina. 'Might be some risk to this,' Kitchim observed, dropping the reins, 'but wherever one can it generally pays to stay within the law. So we'll talk to the man.'

Matching his stride as he moved toward the jail Meetah, looking doubtful, wondered if the law might not be profiting from the steal. 'It's certainly possible,' Kitchim nodded. 'That's the risk I mentioned, and one of the reasons I don't want anyone lighting a shuck out of here. But if we bypass the law and it comes to gunplay—which it probably will, we could find ourselves between two fires, if you know what I mean. Now back my play and let me do the talking.'

She said with her chin up, 'We don't even know they're coming here.'

'They'll be here,' Jeff growled. 'I've got a bet riding on it.'

79

The jail door was open. The first hitch occurred when, within three strides, it became apparent the place held neither jailed nor jailer.

Kitchim swung round. 'Probably wettin' his whistle. Keep behind me when we go in.'

No one in Guerras appeared to mind flies. It was called *The Red Horse* and its door, too, stood wide in invitation. Narrowing his eyes Kitchim slid through the opening, Meetah close on his heels, so close she banged into him when Kitchim dropped anchor. It was all that saved him, the shine-streak of steel chunking into the doorframe with the sound of a rattler.

Kitchim yelled like crazy, knocking Meetah aside and clawing for his gun as Pito—down the length of the bar where he'd been standing with another man—opened up with a pistol. But he was firing too fast, flustered by Jeff's shouts. Kitchim's first shot spun him half around; his second took the other man just above the belt. You could see the fellow cave, both hands grabbing at the front of him, the half-drawn gun dropping uselessly onto the floor, its owner folding after it. Pito, groaning, lost his grip on the bar.

It was over that quick. Jeff never did find out who had thrown the knife.

The barkeep, white-faced and shaking, had both hands above his head, eyes big as saucepans. The girl, when Jeff had chance to notice her, looked like she could use a drink. 'Get some help for that feller,' Kitchim growled at the apron, though it was pretty apparent the man was past earthly aid.

Kitchim went behind the bar and filled two shot glasses, downing one, handing the other to Meetah. 'Throw this into you,' he told her brusquely and, when she had done so, hustled her out. In the street he said, 'Find me one of those boys about the size of that jasper I knocked over first—some fellow who's got something under his hat besides hair.'

Without waiting to see if she were going to or not, he ducked back inside, catching hold of the bartender, hauling him round. 'Which of those birds I shot is the law?'

The man's frightened stare skittered away and came back. Sweat filmed his cheeks. He rubbed a hand across his face. '*Tampoco, señor*—neither one.'

'What! Where is he, then?'

'The law she ees gone to—how you say— veesit sick madre.' He rubbed the flats of his hands against the soiled apron. 'Three horas since—hees primo 'ave come from Porvenir.'

Slick enough, Kitchim thought, seeing again in his head the beefy grin of Teófilo. Decoying the man away from town had been easier and cheaper than courting blackmail trying to buy him. 'Get the clothes off that one,' he growled, pointing at Pito, and went back to the street.

He found Meetah coming up with a tall,

stringy peon who had a cast in one eye. She said, 'This is Eduardo.'

'Good man,' Kitchim nodded, and pointed him toward the door of the cantina. 'I want you to put on the clothes of a robber. They're waiting inside—*andale, hombre*!'

He followed him in and, while the fellow was changing, took the barkeep aside. 'I don't say you're mixed into this but I guess you know what's been going on—with the cows,' he said grimly.

Having no real hope of getting anything Jeff was jubilantly astonished when the fellow, devoutly establishing the Sign, while denying complicity reluctantly admitted an understanding of the situation. It tempted hope in Kitchim his luck might be taking a turn for the better and, crowding this, he said fiercely, 'The young lady you just saw is of the Hacienda Bavinuchi, daughter of Don Luis. In regard for your health tell me quickly and dependably how Bavinuchi cattle have come into and departed this community in recent times.' Lifting the reloaded pistol from his belt Kitchim fingered it suggestively.

The whey-faced wretch bade the Virgin strike him dead if he twisted the truth by so much as a single hair. Everyone knew, he explained, he was just a simple man who took his living from God's charity and could tell no more than he had himself heard, having set forth which he proceeded—interspersed with nervous glances at the snout of Jeff's gun—to describe the regrettable arrangements.

'And this arroyo,' Kitchim pressed, 'where the cows change hands before crossing the river—how do I find it?'

Armed with the information Jeff, beckoning Eduardo, returned to the street where he told the girl, 'We'd best get a move on. The rendezvous is west of town a couple of miles and Teófilo's not likely to be in very good temper if his partners in this venture aren't on hand to take delivery.'

The girl's eyes widened. 'You know the place?'

'Near enough,' Kitchim answered, wondering about Fell who'd been told to keep an eye on Pito and that other one.

Speculation stirred behind her glance when Jeff gruffly bade her gather in the others and he'd catch up with them shortly. 'Walk the horses and don't stir more dust than you have . . . Here—wait!' he growled, having caught sight of Fell propping up the front of the saddle shop yonder. 'You, over there! You look the kind that can take care of himself. Want to earn a few bucks?'

Mattie Fell, pushing erect, shoved himself off the wall, narrowing stare lewdly rummaging the girl in man's pants before reluctantly swiveling his jaw toward Jeff. 'You talkin' at me, mate?' He'd come into the West by way of the Horn and in unguarded moments sometimes dropped a few words he'd picked up while at sea. 'Doin' what?' he said, glowering.

'Helping get back a few cows from some rustlers. Good pay in it for you and maybe a job if you turn out to be as tough as you look.'

Fell's surly stare looked as rough as a cob. 'An' who are you, matey?'

The girl peered more sharply at Jeff when he said, 'Boss of vaqueros for the Hacienda Bavinuchi,' but she kept her thoughts buried. Fell's tone was scornful: 'An I'm Bucky O'Neil! Le's see the color of your dinero if there's more t' this than hogwash.'

Kitchim, considerably riled, was minded to tell the son of a bitch where to go when the girl, cool as a well chain, hauled a poke from her pocket and tossed him a gold piece, arrogant as one scattering pearls before swine.

Fell's jaw dropped but he wasn't above scrounging around in the dust of the road to retrieve it. Kitchim's lip curled but he needed Fell's gun if they were to stop Teófilo and make good his boast. Those peons of Meetah's probably couldn't hit the broad side of a barn! 'You have a horse, hombre?'

'Sure I got a horse.'

'Get on it then and find me a rifle, and find one for yourself if you don't already have one.'

'Takes dinero t' buy rifles.'

'Take 'em out of that twenty if you can't get them no other way,' Jeff said and Fell, grumbling and scowling, took himself off between the ends of two buildings.

'Think he'll come back?' Meetah asked, and Jeff snorted. 'With that gold in his jeans you couldn't keep him away with a carreta of switches!' And, sure enough, before they'd rounded up the rest of their outfit, Mattie Fell appeared on a flax-maned sorrel with the butts of two rifles joggling over his knees.

Kitchim, catching the weapon Fell tossed him, very nearly forgot his great need for this fellow. 'This the rest of your army?' the gunman sneered, eyeing them. Kitchim, inwardly seething, hauled his eyes off the single shot Remington to growl, 'Let's see the one you got,' suspecting from the look of the butt it was a magazine loading U. S. Army .30 caliber. Jeff put out his hand but Fell with a grin sidled his mount out of reach. 'Best I could do fer you, mister. Where-at's them rustlers you want me t'plant?'

'Man could pretty easy wear out his welcome,' Kitchim said thinly. But for the moment, anyway, there wasn't much he could do about it.

Leaving Fell at the head of the column with the girl he pushed on ahead to scout out the place where—according to the barkeep—the transfer of cattle was supposed to come off.

There seemed a better than even chance the guy had lied his damned head off but when Jeff came to the barranca and cautiously quartered it from a brush-shaded rim a child could have guessed cattle had been driven this way more than once. The ground was laced with the marks of their hooves and the droppings he examined were obviously weeks old. Climbing out he beckoned up the others and spied a dust coming out of the wavering south that could hardly be attributable to anything but cattle.

There was plenty of cover along the east rim but the opposite bank stood bare as a bridle, less precipitous too and altogether unsavory from Jeff's turn of mind. Certainly it would prove no obstacle to any bunch of wild critters stampeded by gunfire.

With a jerk of the chin he summoned Fell aside. 'That don't look so good,' the guy muttered, following Jeff's glance. 'Whoever picked this place sure as hell wasn't figgerin' to be sucked into no trap. By the way, who's the filly?'

Kitchim's stare turned ringy. 'That's the old man's daughter. Stay away from her, Fell.'

The gun fighter's glance went over Jeff's shoulder for another brightening look. 'You know me,' he ribbed, 'strictly business an' cash on the barrelhead.'

'I won't tell you again.'

Fell, brashly grinning, dug Jeff in the ribs. 'In a pardnership deal it's share an' share a—'

Jeff's whistling fist, exploding against the bones of the man's face, took Fell out of the saddle as though driven headlong into the jut of a limb.

He lit heavily, spraddled out, and took his time getting up, looking meaner than fish eggs rolled in sand, Too late, staring into that ugly regard, Kitchim realized the depth if not the scope of his mistake. Still riled, breathing hard, he made no attempt to assuage the man's feelings, knowing such an effort would be taken by Fell for either weakness or fear.

Instead he said like he was talking to dirt, 'Don't put your mouth to her again.'

CHAPTER THIRTEEN

The ambush was organized with dispatch, care and all the cold-blooded purpose a man of Jeff's experience could bring to a task demanding so large a division of authority among so motley a crew. Each of them had his job and was painstakingly rehearsed for precision and savvy, not even the girl being left out of these arrangements. So few to throw against so many, the odds being feverishly against his objective when balanced in comparative quality as respecting the caliber of the two opposing teams.

He dared not count on the girl yet was forced to—the same applying to any help he might expect from Fell.

The six peons from Bavinuchi were probably loyal but ignorant, untrained and untried, not used to thinking for themselves, unskilled in the use of either arms or horses. He dismounted and scattered them in the brush of the east rim with their repeated instructions and hodgepodge of weaponry—all but the judas goat, the man picked to play the role of Pito.

This one with Meetah, who might pass in the fellow's hat for Pito's erstwhile companion, he posted beside a small hastily arranged fire built in the ashes of an older one in the barranca itself, off to one side of the hoof-gouged trail in a rubble of fallen rock. With them he placed Fell, and their trio of horses he ground-hitched nearby. To further this appearance of encampment boredom he had the girl with her hidden hair pushed up under the hat hunkered beside the fire with Eduardo—the one garbed as Pito—busied with a skillet. Fell sullenly slouched nearby on a rock, rifle concealed behind an outstretched leg. All the rest of the horses were tied back out of sight.

'The idea,' Kitchim murmured, 'is to fetch Teófilo and most of his helpers as close to this point as can be before I start the ball rolling.' Eyeing Meetah, he said, 'At the first hint of gunplay you drop flat on the ground.'

Glancing again toward the dust, which seemed now scarcely more than a half mile away, Jeff picked up his single-shot Remington and stepped behind a brush-fringed boulder directly confronting the approach of the herd.

He was resigned to a stampede, knowing the cows would inevitably bolt that low and easily scaled west bank. What he hoped to prevent was the escape of the robbers; he'd instructed his companions to drop as many as possible, specifically directing Fell with his repeater to make sure of the big-bellied foreman in the event, through some fluke, Jeff failed in this himself.

With nothing to do now but wait and hope Kitchim, able from his position to keep an eye on the three by the fire, had plenty of time to regret the mad impulse that had made him tie into Fell the way he had. The man's allegiance at best had been highly problematical. There was now no telling what the fellow might do. He'd be plagued by the need to get back at Jeff—might even tell Meetah what Kitchim was up to as a means of getting even while advancing his chances to climb into Jeff's boots. He had the bone-seasoned look of this kind of a bastard. Only the man's inbred caution gave Jeff any hope at all, and it was hardly a thing a guy would want to sink or swim by.

Kitchim could not think what had set him off, why he'd reacted with such violence to the man's salacious gabble. The girl was nothing but a pawn in the high stakes game Jeff was

89

playing. If he was minded to marry her it was not for the lure of any roll in the hay but strictly as a means of arriving more surely—more advantageously—at the goal already hung up for himself.

He could hear the hooves, the clack of horns, and peering through the yellowing fronds of salt cedar he saw the lead riders with the van of the herd lumbering into plain sight against the pall of dun dust being raised by their passage. He got down behind his rock, sleeving the sweat from his eyes, rubbing the palms of his hands against his thighs. Once he'd fired its one shot this rifle was useless. He had no reloads, which was the principal reason for wanting this bunch to come up close where he'd have at least a chance of maybe scoring with his pistol.

He heard Teófilo's lusty yell sail through the rumble of hooves; saw Eduardo straighten out of his crouch and half turn by the fire to wave before setting his empty skillet aside, its emptiness being another piece of carelessness Kitchim should have noticed and corrected, but the breeze, at least, was luckily blowing from the herd, so maybe it wouldn't matter that there was no smell of frying meat in the air.

And perhaps, in itself, this wouldn't have mattered. But there were other small lacks, insignificant alone but breeding in the aggregate an atmosphere at variance with the feel Jeff had tried to build into this camp scene. Teófilo a hundred yards away commenced to frown and fan his eyes about.

The next hitch occurred when Eduardo, rising, put the side of his face with the white eye forward and Teófilo—now barely fifty yards from the fire—threw up a hand to warn his outfit; and the fitful breeze chose that moment to send Meetah's borrowed hat kiting, dumping that mane of black hair about her shoulders.

With a snarl the boss vaquero—as Eduardo froze—spun his horse on hind legs and Jeff, that instant firing, missed, to frustratedly watch the yelling Mexican, flat against his barreling mount, go streaking up that broken west bank in the van of the herd's wild bolt from flame-gouting brush and the crack-crack of rifles.

The place was a bedlam of frenzied confusion crammed with the bawling of terrified cattle and the cries and shouts of frantic men. Kitchim, dropping the Remington, grabbed up his pistol and, charging into the open, ran cursing and firing after the fleeing vaqueros, hearing the steady vicious racket of Fell's smoke-wreathed repeater.

Three spurring riders clawed the crumbling bank, made it to the top and fell back as though cut from their saddles by the swing of some monstrous unseen scythe. One riderless mount, reins flying, achieved comparative safety, only to go screaming up on hind feet and collapse in a thrashing blood-gouting fall.

It was over that sudden.

Jeff, numb in the backwash of that mad din, looked around at the huddled lumps of dead bodies. He was not one to retch, but the need churned through him, brassy as bile. Someone moved out yonder, feebly throwing up a hand. Fell's rifle cracked and the shape collapsed. More than anything else this kicked up Jeff's fury, the callous wantonness of it stirring all his frustrations,

Yet he kept his lip buttoned, the surging temper locked back of grinding teeth.

There were seven dead riders, two dead peons and three others who'd been nicked or creased but could still sit a saddle well enough to get on with it. They were faced with the task of rounding up the cows. He saw the girl's worried look but, ignoring it, dropped back to ride with Fell when they set out through the lengthening shadows reaching down from the hills to see how many they could find.

'When we gettin' down t' cases?' Fell growled. 'Straightaway.' The two governments involved, Kitchim told him, by the treaty of 1905 had agreed that all parcels of land moved by shifting channels from one side of the river to the other should be regarded, while remaining in these new positions, as land ceded by the loser to the country now possessing them—ownership, however, to remain in the hands of the original proprietors unless they refused citizenship or otherwise disposed of same.

'An' how does that help us?' Fell grumbled.

'Do you think a lone female, or a girl with a sick dad—stuck with riders she can't depend on, is fixed to put up much of a fuss against a pair of tough gringos determined to take over?'

Fell, scowling, said, 'Well, but . . . Hell's fire! You don't even know there's gonna *be* a new channel—'

'There'll be one, all right. That's where you come in, but there'll be one if I have to dig it myself.'

'Dig?' Fell said, and stared open-mouthed. 'Y' mean I'm supposed t' dig it? Jesus Christ, man—'

'It ain't all that rough,' Kitchim said with curled lip. 'There's a natural valley swings. All we need's about forty foot of bed and a good charge of sticks to blow her in. Day after tomorrow I'll give you a look at it. All we'll need is a storm to make it look good and, come the next morning, Bavinuchi'll wake up to find it's part of Texas. Put your mind to it, feller. There we'll be, tucked in pretty as two sixshooters riding the same belt.'

Kitchim reckoned he may have over-simplified it somewhat, but in a hurried-up view this was the plan he carried in his head, this was the long-nourished blueprint for success on which he was staking his life's biggest gamble. And he didn't, by God, see how it could miss. The deflection of the river into the trough of that valley would require nothing more than he had told Fell it would; forty feet of twenty-foot channel and about ten sticks of dynamite. It wasn't deflecting the channel that worried him, it was the matter of female unreasonableness, the femaleness of viewing every brought-up thing or subject as they wanted to see it. Logic meant nothing at all to a woman and he was far from convinced, once they'd changed the channel, Meetah Capistrano could be made to realize she had lost Bavinuchi.

The harder he looked at this business of Meetah the more inclined Kitchim was to re-evaluate his hand. And he didn't have to study his cards much to see that the best way around her was a trip in double harness.

For a while as the hours dragged past he considered the possibilities of conversational wedlock, of simply leading her to *think* it was the object of his court; and with some women a deal of that kind might have worked, the final disillusionment knocking the fight all out of them.

He couldn't believe it would with Meetah. Certainly not while Teófilo was still around to be bargained with! Or Fell and his cupidity! As long as she had one fist left she'd fight!

Fiercely scowling Kitchim reckoned the surest and shortest way to Bavinuchi was to marry the ranch.

CHAPTER FOURTEEN

It wasn't like she was ugly, one-legged or purely given to running-off at the mouth. Or because she was Mex—he didn't care about that. He could still feel the pull of her burning all through him, making scriggly prickles flush up and down his spine. But a man liked to figure he wore the pants in his family and with a filly like Meetah you couldn't ever be more than twenty per cent sure.

They got the cows home, the big bulk of them anyhow, Teófilo powerfully conspicuous by the fact of his absence—not once had they crossed even a sign of the man. Nor was Kitchim misled into thinking he'd seen the last of the fellow. He could not be even reasonably certain the three or four hombres who had disappeared with him had not since returned to be caught up in the chores he handed out each morning as boss of vaqueros.

The first thing he'd done after being named foreman was to make a brief to-do of elevating Eduardo—the man who'd played Pito at the camp in the barranca—to the post of segundo, second in command, an innovation little relished by the rank and file of riders who, although under orders, liked to look upon themselves as considerably better than mere peons.

Kitchim, despite their dark looks, went ahead with it anyway, wanting—regardless of shortcomings—to feel he'd have one man whose loyalty he could count on. Fell he took on as hired gun, ostensibly as insurance against rustlers. 'You won't 'ave to show up every night at headquarters if it should seem inconvenient—I'll cover you there,' Jeff said while they were riding out a few days later to have a look at Fell's project. 'May take a week or so to get through with that digging. I'll fetch a couple peons out with tools and grub tomorrow. We're coming into the time of rain. The sooner you get the thing ready the better.'

Fell, scowling, grunted. 'Seems,' he mentioned after mulling it over, 'I'm gettin' stuck with the heavy end of this,' and considered Jeff dourly. 'You sure I'm down in your books fer half?'

Kitchim, catching the hard glint of Fell's probing stare, said, 'I don't hardly see how I could cross you up short of bringin' this to gunplay.'

'See that you remember it—I don't figger to be caught nappin,' Fell snarled in a blustery tone.

That night Jeff told Meetah, 'We could do with a few dug tanks on this spread. Think I'll take a couple of your boys out tomorrow and look around. Any runoff we catch from the rains, if we could store it, would open up—'

She said, apparently uninterested in the details of ranch managment, 'I think you'd better send someone for that doctor again.'

'Your father's worse?'

'I don't know that he's worse. He doesn't seem much better.' She said broodingly, 'That arm is still stiff. I can't seem to make out half he says anymore and sometimes . . . sometimes I don't think he hears me at all.'

'I'll send someone straightaway,' Jeff said, but she caught at his hand. 'Tomorrow will do.' Her eyes searched his queerly. 'Have you known many women?'

What was a fellow supposed to make out of that? Kitchim peered at her uneasily. 'I've known a few,' he said gruffly.

'Were they prettier than I?'

'Dance-hall women most of them,' Jeff growled. Then he scraped up the nerve to say, 'I've never known a girl like you before,' and waited, scarce breathing, to see how it hit her.

She seemed almost to stop breathing too for a moment. Then she dropped his hand and stepped back. 'I must go now.'

The Doc, when he came, had very little to say. Jeff wasn't around but Meetah told him later it was the medico's opinion her father's chances of recovery were hardly worth discussing, that another stroke would kill him.

The girl sighed. 'He's to be kept warm, kept in bed, and to avoid excitement.' She appeared pretty gloomy.

Kitchim, sorry for her but behind this surface sympathy jubilant at the upswing in prospects her words seemed to herald, caught hold of her impulsively. Bone deep in his own needs he said with the words tumbling over each other, 'It's too much for a girl to be forced to shoulder . . . all this trouble over the cows, that crazy Teófilo stirring up discontent—in his need for revenge plotting only the Lord knows what kind of devilment, and your father in no shape to comfort or help. Marry me, Meetah! Let me take care of—'

The torrent of words piled up in his throat. Aghast he peered at the enormous eyes staring back at him, at the shock and astonishment so nakedly apparent . . . the stiffening composure glaring through this incredulity as breeding and background stirred gathering flecks of scorn and indignation into the coalescing fusion of a fiercening resentment.

Suddenly appalled at his temerity Kitchim grabbed his hat and stumbled from the room.

*   *   *

During the weeks that followed while the ditch was being dug, Kitchim, up to his ears in the thousand and one details of managing a ranch of Bavinuchi's magnitude, saw little of the girl, discovering no chance of talking with her alone. Teófilo had disappeared as though the very bowels of the earth had opened up to swallow him.

Jeff, keeping in touch with what transpired in the house through conversations conducted with the servants by Eduardo, learned of Don Luis' continuing decline. The master of Bavinuchi on a diet of broths no longer concerned himself with matters of this planet, the segundo reported. Shrunken beyond belief, Jeff was told, the old man lay in a kind of trance, perhaps communing with God.

'He is not long for this world,' Eduardo said, piously crossing himself to ward off bad luck. 'The señorita? A-a-aí-hé! She is sad and pale like a wilted flower. She sits all the time by the bed watching, I think, for el hombre of the Black Horse.'

It was hard for Jeff to picture her so. She had seemed so alive, so crammed with life's juices. He cursed himself for a bungling fool. If he'd been content to let well enough alone . . . Well, no matter, he thought, anxiously scanning the skies, his original plan was as good now as ever. Fell's ditch was almost ready. Thrown back on his former intention he found it difficult to see—surrounded as she was by the hacienda's isolations—what the heir to Bavinuchi could do to circumvent him. He could keep her a prisoner indefinitely if he had to.

The mayordomo? Kitchim's lips twisted. Another doddering ancient with his snags of bad teeth and silly half senile chuckles. He had nothing to fear from a man who spent most of his few wakeful hours waylaying opportunities for pinching girls' bottoms. The reins of government were in Kitchim's hands.

It would have to rain sometime. One good storm plus those little yellow sticks would lift the river from its channel.

But he didn't know about the fat-bellied man keeping tab on Fell's progress from the cover of the hills . . .

In the shank of an afternoon three days later the first fat drops fell out of wind-tossed clouds to lance the smoky film of heat and thwack against the drought-parched earth with the spattering force of liquid hail. The peons looked up with gleeful grins, riders went phlegmatically about their chores and half an hour later the sun broke through, much to Kitchim's disgust.

Two thunder showers, six hours apart, raced across the thirsty earth the next day, neither of them robust enough to develop any lengthy stands of water. Fell rode in about dark, grinning hugely. 'Must've had a real gully washer north of here someplace. River's up three foot an' still risin'. There's a soft spot in that stretch we left. Ditch is ready—why not blow her tonight?'

Kitchim eyed him tight-lipped. 'Keep your

voice down, you fool! You want to tell the whole country?'

'Hell, these peons—'

'The crew just rode in. They're already curious—'

'An' small wonder,' Fell flared, 'the way you've had 'em shiftin' cattle ag'in' the river this last week—I been some curious myself. What you tryin' t' do—put 'em *all* on this banco?'

Jeff had told him not to use that word around headquarters and this aggravation, topping the suspicion in the man's tone and eyes, made it hard to keep his hands off the fellow. Grinding down on his rage he growled, 'Don't bother unsaddling. We're going back out there.'

A hot wind blew the length of the valley. Fell against orders had come in that way and was aware that Jeff knew this. With his hat pushed back the rusty red of his hair matched the jerky brightness looking out of that too narrow, too foxy, slanch of eyes.

He was like a spring wound too right, and the look of him warned Kitchim the tiger-faced Texan had more on his mind than that disreputable hat. He could feel the excitement churning back of Fell's stare, as now the man said, 'We ain't goin' t' need fifty riders once we cut this chunk off from the rest of it. All the shots are in place. It's goin' t' storm again t'night, so how's about takin' half the crew along with us?'

'I don't quite catch the drift of it,' Jeff said.

'A lot of them fellers ain't goin' t' be too happy when they find this spread's become a part of Texas. Time t' get shut of 'em's right now before we blow it. An' we ain't got much time—river's eatin' into that bank right now.'

'Guess I'm too pooped to cope with riddles, Matt. Just say right out what you've got in mind.'

'Look,' Fell said. 'Be a deal of confusion— bound t' be. Right? We don't want anyone draggin' their feet, that's fer sure. Some of these hombres is goin' t' resent you bein' put over 'em—hell, a lot of these Mexicans got no use fer Americans. My idee, once we've blown in this banco, is keep the girl under wraps until she signs the spread over, an' we don't want around a lot of yaps that'd take up f' her. *I* say git rid of 'em before they git their backs up or open their mouths.'

'And how do we do this?'

'Show 'em that cut. Git 'em pokin' round in it and then blow the whole works.'

Kitchim's stomach turned over. Yet he wasn't—not really—too terribly astonished. To the gun fighter's conscienceless warped way of thinking this cold-blooded proposal offered a logical solution to the control of Bavinuchi. And he was obviously pleased with himself for having hit on it. What occupied Jeff was the way this spelled out the big difference between them . . . and the uncomfortable picture the man's words set up of how far down the no-return trail he'd come himself. There was no essential difference between what Fell had in mind for Meetah and the way Jeff had figured on handling her.

Forgotten was the river and self interest as Kitchim, like a man shaken out of a dream, looked around and saw himself as he most probably looked to others. He didn't like what he saw and shook his head as though to change it, hearing the gun fighter stir and clear his throat with some impatience.

The fishbelly shine of those grinning eyes reminded Jeff that Fell was waiting for some expression of approval. What could he say to him—what *dared* he say?

To give himself time to iron out his own thinking he said, 'Maybe I will take a few of them out there. Not too many. When we move this deal into Texas we want a strong enough crew to make sure we hang onto it. Wait here. I'll see what I can come up with.'

He strode off into the dark, the feel of the man's eyes stabbing into his back like the jab of steel needles.

He was too torn with doubts to think clearly, running into blank walls every way he turned. It wasn't just Fell or that greedy Texas marshal that bothered him half as much as did the pictures he kept seeing of that ▓▓dam girl.

Turning into the lamplit mess shack his

glance quartered over the hands who'd come in, primarily looking for men he believed would stick with the ranch if anything came up which might tend to test loyalties. He reckoned four would be enough to handle the vague and still tentative notion that kept sliding around through the churn of his thoughts, and gave his selections the nod as he made them. The four followed him out.

In the starlight he said, 'We're ridin'. It could be a rough trip so pick the best, freshest mounts you can put your ropes on.'

He could feel their curiosity as they moved toward the pens. They asked no questions. When they'd caught their mounts, the saddling completed they looked to him for orders. Kitchim growled at them gruffly, 'You may see some queer things where we're fixin' to go. You are not under orders. You will do what you think—each in his own heart—is best for Bavinuchi. Without regard for anything else. Is—'

A sound no louder than the snapping of a stick jerked Jeff's chin toward the windows of the house. Only one of these showed light, and most of this was filtered through a screen of bougainvillea. 'Stay put!' Kitchim grunted, and broke into a run, knowing that sound for the report of a shot.

The guard had come out of his box at the gate to peer open-mouthed toward that one spot of light. Kitchim, rattling the grill, thought the fool would never turn. *'Let me through!'* he snarled, and was bitterly afraid, mind leaping ahead with its visions of Teófilo as he tore through the tangle of foliage that separated him from the portal.

The door was open, and the door beyond. Over the heads of a goggling huddle of servants, gun still in hand, he could see Mattie Fell with his wolflike grin closing in on the girl. He had her backed into an angle of the patio wall. The knife in her hand was all that kept Fell from grabbing her.

To take the girl out of line Jeff was forced to move in from the side. He dared not take his eyes from the man. Yet so engrossed was Fell it wasn't until Jeff thumbed back the hammer of his pistol that the gun fighter suddenly awoke to his peril.

He spun like a cat, eyes slitted, gun lifting in a burst of livid flame. One of those slugs flung Kitchim half around. Then his own gun spoke. Fell's eyes went wide and you could see shock travel all through his face, and like that he stood perhaps another half minute. With a terrible effort he tried to bring up his gun. His legs let go and he pitched suddenly forward, dead before he struck. Only then did Kitchim notice Don Luis' crumpled shape with the blood pooling round it.

The girl, he saw, was on the verge of hysteria. He caught hold of her, shook her. 'It's time you learned,' he growled, 'life's no bowl of g̶o̶d̶dam roses!' and slapped her stingingly across both cheeks. She tried to use the knife she still held and he cuffed it, clattering, into the fountain. Nodding, he said, 'That's better—come on!'

She was like a child in his grip, her resistance ridiculous. When she saw how useless it was she quit struggling and presently, breathless, found herself at the gate.

The guard let them through. A look at Jeff's face left the questions piled up behind his scared stare. Meetah, hustled along in Kitchim's fiercening grip, arrived at the corrals and saw the shadowy shapes of waiting men. 'She goes with us,' Kitchim said. 'José', give the lady your horse—you stay here.'

In the saddle Meetah said, 'Where are you taking me?'

'Perhaps to see the end of a world.'

Tearing through the black night with its drizzle of rain he didn't know himself what he might finally do. All his values were unsettled and the notions now haring around in their place he couldn't understand. It seemed crazy to throw away all he had worked for . . . he didn't know if he could do it.

He spoke abruptly to the girl. 'Do you know what a banco is?'

She shook her head—he could see that much. 'You stand a damn good chance of bein' on one before morning.' Gruffly then he told her of the treaty between the United States and Mexico whereby one stood to lose what the other gained as a result of the Rio Grande changing its bed. 'Would you swear allegiance to the gringo flag?'

'I would have to think about it. Why is this important?'

'The river's up. The west bank, where we're going, looks in danger of being undercut. A lot of that rock has turned out to be rotten. Fell's had two of your paisanos working there, making a ditch.'

The girl, saying nothing, continued to watch him as the horses took them into heavier rain. 'A ditch,' Kitchim growled, 'that'll bring the Rio rolling down this trough an' practically into Bavinuchi's back yard.'

Soaked to the skin they huddled in the leathers while the floundering horses carried them north and east and the rain drummed into the slickening earth. She was silent so long Jeff reckoned she hadn't heard or couldn't make out the significance of what he'd said.

She'd understood right enough, had probably caught every word. The trust in her reply while she peered through the dark was like a knife turning in him, its bite slicing deeper than the slug from Fell's gun. She said, 'You'll know how it happened. You can tell them the truth.'

Lightning skipped along the rim of the world, distant thunder rolled through the rain and the ground was a sea of glistening mud.

The horses, floundering now, seemed to spend half their strength trying to keep legs under them and you could feel the strain in their trembling flanks.

The cold of the night got into Jeff's bones. A gust of wind slammed against them and the slog of the rain was like a pounding from fists, beating Jeff into the trap of his thoughts. *Bavinuchi!* he snarled, and it was like a curse, as though he were beginning to wish he'd never heard of the place.

Some might think this a pretty barren region to be getting so worked up about, but never a man who knew the West. Desolate, remote, uncultured and uncared for—it was all of these, and vast and still, crammed with dangers and steeped in violence, too hot and too bright with its barbaric vistas and sand-scoured heights, its fierce winds and cruel droughts, flash floods and storms that could boil out of nowhere and in a matter of minutes wipe away a life's work. It was cattle land, cow country, good for man and good for beast. Even cut in half by the river—as Kitchim planned—the hacienda could be made to support every critter he'd gathered, including horses. Too much to give up for a crazy whim! For a girl who thought him no better than dirt!

She could never hang onto it—no woman could.

There was more lightning now, great sizzling bolts of it ripping open the skies, the heavy tumble of thunder seeming almost incessant. It was hard to guess how far they had come but they must, Kitchim reckoned, be getting close to that ditch. And then, in an unconscionably bright, all-encompassing flash the whole world seemed to explode. Shocked and gasping they pulled up, numbly staring at each other. 'Was that thunder?' Meetah cried in a jumpety voice.

Through the drumming of rain a new sound swelled like wind ballooning into a monstrous roar. In a lurid flash Kitchim saw it—a solid twenty-foot wall of churning water rushing toward them out of the rain-lashed night.

'The river!' Kitchim shouted, swinging his rein-ends at the rump of Meetah's terrified horse. 'Out of here—*out!*' he yelled, spurring frantically after her.

The horses needed no urging. Ears flattened, eyes rolling, they lunged from the trough. Slipping, sliding, twisting and squealing in the suck of that muck, they floundered, spent and wheezing, onto high ground.

'There's no good—' Jeff began, and let the words fall away as he followed, with rain-blurred stare, the rigid stretch of a vaquero's arm.

Three riders, head on, were pounding out of the storm, a dark huddle of shapes in the slant of the rain until a jagged lemon flash limned them stark for what they were. The burly shoulders of the man in the middle—the lead rider—grabbed all of Jeff's attention. The streaming patch and flash of teeth behind the bristle of ragged mustachios brought a shout of 'Teófilo!' churning up out of him as he clawed for his gun.

The jump of the butt kicking hard at his palm was a beautiful feeling—but a greater satisfaction boiled through his veins when he saw the renegade reel in his saddle and with outflung arms go ass-over-elbows off the back of his mount.

They were all firing now and, that quick, it was finished.

* * *

In the receding rumble of departing thunder the sound of the river was a grinding roar, filling their minds with its tumult and import. Kitchim's banco now was an established fact, but there was no triumph in him, just the bitter taste of a despair he could not fathom.

Perhaps, in part, the loss of blood from the bite of Fell's slug had something to do with this wrung-out feeling; he hardly seemed his usual self, but a bullet creased biceps wasn't serious enough to fill his head with the kind of damned bilge he was finding there.

He looked around through the slackening thinness of rain and disgustedly blew some of the drip off his nose. 'We might as well go back.'

No one raised any objections.

Kitchim found himself someway paired off with the girl and it was Meetah who presently broke the morose silence he seemed to have built around him. 'I had never dreamed to find Bavinuchi a part of Texas.'

He said nothing to that.

But she was not discouraged. Stars were beginning to liven up the black and as the trail took them farther from the sound of the river and the grunting racket of gleeful frogs, still eyeing him she said in a thoughtful tone of voice, 'You weren't planning to quit, were you?'

'I'd probably better,' he grumbled. 'You don't need me—'

'But without you to show me, how would I ever keep the rest of those Texans from stealing Bavinuchi?'

The old pull was still there. Kitchim scowled at her irritably. 'It wasn't Fell that was planning to steal it—it was *me*,' he said bluntly.

'How very enterprising of you. And how did you think to ever get title, or hadn't you gotten that far?' she asked coolly.

'I was going to shut you up somewhere till you signed the place over.'

She put her head on one side. 'I could fall in love with a man that resourceful.'

'A gringo?' Kitchim said, staring.

The gamin grin crossed her lips. 'You might stay around and find out,' she suggested.

We hope you have enjoyed this Large Print book. Other Chivers Press or Thorndike Press Large Print books are available at your library or directly from the publishers.

For more information about current and forthcoming titles, please call or write, without obligation, to:

Chivers Press Limited
Windsor Bridge Road
Bath BA2 3AX
England
Tel. (01225) 335336

OR

G.K. Hall & Co.
295 Kennedy Memorial Drive
Waterville
Maine 04901
USA

All our Large Print titles are designed for easy reading, and all our books are made to last.